THE
DANCE
OF
GENGHIS COHN

THE
DANCE
OF
GENGHIS COHN

ROMAIN GARY

JONATHAN CAPE
THIRTY BEDFORD SQUARE
LONDON

PRINTED IN GREAT BRITAIN BY
COMPTON PRINTING LTD, AYLESBURY
ON PAPER MADE BY JOHN DICKINSON & CO. LTD
BOUND BY A. W. BAIN & CO. LTD, LONDON

CONTENTS

PART THREE — THE TEMPTATION OF GENGHIS COHN

THE
DANCE
OF
GENGHIS COHN

PART
ONE

THE
DYBBUK

1.

Allow Me
to Introduce
Myself

I feel at home here. I feel part of the place and of the very
air they breathe, in a way that only those who have been
completely naturalized and thoroughly assimilated can understand. A sort of clamoring absence. The absence is so in-
sistent, so overwhelming, that it becomes almost a presence.
Of course, there's been some wear and tear, through ignorance, familiarity, and loss of memory—time has a way of
cleansing a place better than rats and you can't expect the
German sky to wear the yellow Star of David forever. Temporarily darkened by the Jewish smoke, the blue beast of
eternity rubs a little wind over its mug and everything is
beautiful again. I'm sensitive to beauty, to perfection. As I
float around, lolling on my back, twiddling my thumbs—eternity's favorite pastime—I'm filled with wonder at this immaculate purity around me. All this radiant gold and blue makes
me think of the madonna of the frescoes, of the fairy princess
in the legends. The sky is a great artist.

Allow me to introduce myself: the name is Cohn, Genghis
Cohn: my real name was Moishe, but Genghis went better
with my rather wild stage personality. I'm a comedian, and

in the old days I used to be very well known on the Yiddish burlesque circuit: first at the Shwarze Shikse, in Berlin, then at the Mottke Ganeff in Warsaw, and finally in Auschwitz. I don't know if you are old enough to remember me, but those who do will tell you, I'm sure, how much I used to make them laugh. It's true that many people objected to my brand of humor. They often felt shocked and shaken and some critics expressed strong reservations about my act: they thought that it lacked dignity. My wit, or *khokhme,* as we call it, they found either too arrogant or too self-deprecating, either too biting and cruel or, on the contrary, self-pitying and close to black despair. One of the critics wrote in the *Nasz Przeglad* of Warsaw: "Mr. Genghis Cohn's humor occasionally sounds like some kind of helpless and hopeless self-defense. This comedian seems unable to find a middle ground between a sort of Jewish Uncle-Tomism and hostility, often sinking to downright provocation and abuse."

Even my friends advised me to be a little less aggressive: there was already enough anti-Semitism around. Maybe they were right. In Auschwitz, one day, I told a fellow inmate such a funny joke that he literally died laughing. He was undoubtedly the only Jew who ever died laughing in Auschwitz. The German guards were furious.

I myself didn't stay in that famous camp very long, escaping miraculously in December 1943, God be praised, only to be recaptured a few months later by SS troops under *Hauptjudenfresser* Schatz. I call him Schatzchen in private, an endearing word meaning "little precious one," and for centuries part of German lovers' vocabulary. Schatzchen is today the police commissioner here in Licht. As a matter of fact, that's why I am here in Licht myself. I follow him around. We're great buddies.

I must say that nature is lovely here, and I could have done much worse. Some of us have been naturalized and assimilated in all kinds of unpleasant surroundings. But this place is delightful. Woods, streams, chirping robins, wild geese *und ruhig fliesst der Rhein, die schönsten Jungfrauen sitzet dort ober wunderbar, ihr' goldene geschmeide glitzet, sie kämmt ihre goldene hahr* . . . Heine's *Lorelei*. I'm very fond of poetry.

We became inseparable, Schatzchen and I, on a certain beautiful, cold day of April 1944. Schatz has sheltered me ever since: for almost twenty-four years he's been hiding a Jew. I try not to take advantage of his hospitality, not to take up too much room. People often say that we're pushing, give us a finger and we grab the whole hand, and so I try to show them how discreet and tactful we can be. I always leave him alone in the bathroom, and when he has a romance under way I'm very careful not to show up at an awkward moment. When two people have to live so close together, discretion and restraint are essential.

Which reminds me that I've been neglecting Schatzchen a bit this past half-hour. It's true he's very busy right now, with all these terrible murders that have plunged the whole region of Licht into fear and indignation. But that's no reason to neglect a friend. I'm sure he can do with a little moral support.

So I have decided to manifest myself, as I always do when Schatzchen is overworked and nervous. I usually like to make a striking, dramatic appearance: it's the old ham in me. But I resist the temptation: this is not a time to drive him nuts. I therefore proceed as discreetly as I can to Police Headquarters, 12 Goethestrasse.

There's a mob of reporters waiting in the street, but nobody notices me nowadays. I'm no longer news, the public has had enough of me, they simply don't want to hear about me anymore. The young people particularly couldn't care less. They're bored to tears by the war veterans' rambling tales of their heroic deeds. "Papa's Jews," they call us.

I slip inside and lean with solicitude over my friend's shoulder. He stirs uneasily, but I don't insist and he remains unaware of my presence.

Poor Schatzchen is very, very tired. He's had almost no sleep at all the last three nights, and he drinks too much. He's got to watch himself. He's not that young anymore and with all the *tsuris* I've given him, he might easily have a heart attack. I must be careful. I don't want to lose a man who has sheltered me for so many years. I don't know at all what would become of me without him.

The office is very clean: my friend has an obsession about cleanliness. He's constantly washing his hands: a nervous tic. He's even had a little sink installed under the official portrait of President Luebke. Every few minutes or so he gets up to make his ablutions. He uses a special powder for this. Never soap. Schatzchen has a real phobia about soap. He says some of the old wartime soaps are still around and you never know with *whom* you are dealing.

The Commissioner's secretary sits behind a small desk at the back of the room, busily writing a report about the latest murder. Hübsch is his name. He's a mournful-looking individual, with prematurely thinning crew-cut hair of the same slightly piggish color as his complexion. His eyes survey the world through a pair of pince-nez that seem to go all the way back to *Simplicissimus* and the good old days of imperial bureaucracy. He's entirely unaware of my presence, or of my absence, whichever you prefer. It was another Hübsch just like this one who, in 1944, wrote out my last identity paper: a death certificate. *Moishe Cohn,* known as *Genghis Cohn. Geboren:* 1912. *Gestorben:* 1944. That, you may notice, makes me exactly thirty-two. If you were born in 1912, thirty-

6

two, that's not bad at all, considering that we're in 1968. That was Christ's age: an interesting coincidence. I often think of Christ. I'm very fond of youth.

Inspector Guth, one of the bright new boys of the Police Department, is talking to the Commissioner. Apparently two local personalities, of considerable importance, both of them influential members of the Christian Democratic Party, wish to see him. Schatzchen won't hear of it. Too busy. I feel a bit sorry for him. He looks exhausted, almost at the end of his rope. We don't want to have another nervous breakdown, do we? That would be bad for our career.

As he grows older, Schatzchen's hope of getting rid of me has shrunk to the point of total despair. He's beginning to understand that nothing can ever separate us. He hardly sleeps at all and I have to spend my nights sitting on his bed, with my yellow star, looking soulfully into his eyes. He particularly hates it when I suggest that we should hold hands. The other night he began to mutter something about "Jewish atrocities." The more exhausted he is, the more obsessive my presence becomes. I don't particularly enjoy keeping him company. But I can't help it. It's all his own doing. It has been my fate to add a new dimension to the legend of the Wandering Jew: that of the immanent Jew, omnipresent, entirely assimilated, forever part of each atom of the German earth, air, and conscience. All I need is a pair of wings and a little pink ass to become a beautiful Jewish angel. You are probably familiar with the new twist given to our old saying in all the *Bierstuben* around Buchenwald, when a sudden silence falls in the conversation: *A Jew is passing by.*

Enough about me. My darling Schatz refuses to see the two "influential gentlemen" who are waiting outside, and that's the end of it.

"I told you, Guth: nobody. I don't want to see a soul."

Nobody? I'm a little hurt, but we'll take care of that.

7

"Tell 'em I've got to give all my attention to these murders. Surely they've heard about them? The papers talk about nothing else."

He grabs the bottle of schnapps on the desk and pours himself a drink. He drinks a lot. It's a tribute to which I am particularly sensitive.

"Baron von Pritwitz is one of the most powerful men in the country," says Guth. "He owns half the Ruhr."

"I don't give a damn."

He takes another drink. Now I'm beginning to worry: the son of a bitch is trying to get rid of me.

Guth is clearly troubled. "And what about the press? They've been waiting all night."

"I'm not going to talk to them. First they accuse the police of incompetence, then when we come up with a suspect—the shepherd who found the last body—they accuse us of looking for a scapegoat."

Guth makes a gesture of helplessness. I like that gesture in a representative of authority. When the police admit their impotence, there's hope. I suddenly experience a strong yen to eat a *rakhat loukoum*. I'm going to ask Schatzchen to run out and buy me some. He never refuses me a little treat. His efforts to please me in the hope of pacifying me are very touching. The other day something rather funny happened. It was Hanukkah and Schatz, whom I have taught all our Jewish holidays, had whipped up a few of my favorite kosher dishes. He had put them on a tray, together with a small bunch of violets in a glass, and had gotten down on his knees to make me the offering. It's a friendly little ritual we have worked out between ourselves, which he scrupulously performs on the eve of every Sabbath and holiday. He has hidden a Jewish calendar in his medicine chest and consults it nervously, lest he forget one of our religious feasts: the last thing he wants is to upset me. He also keeps there a copy of *Aunt*

8

Sarah's Jewish Cookbook. Just at that moment, our landlady, Frau Müller, happened to walk in, and the sight of Police Commissioner *Erste Klasse* Schatz on his knees, beating his chest and presenting a tray of cholent and gefilte fish to a Jew who wasn't there, gave her such a fright that she almost fainted. Since then she avoids Schatz and tells everyone that the Commissioner has gone mad, *erste Klasse* mad. Naturally, nobody understands the kind of relationship we have, which is very special, very fine. We've been inseparable for so long that we have built up together a secret little world all our own, into which it is very difficult to penetrate, unless you happen to be one of the initiated. Schatz gives every sign of having formed a strong sentimental attachment to me, but I'm not a bit fooled by it. I know that he goes to see a psychiatrist, secretly and regularly, in a dastardly attempt to get rid of me. The bastard thinks I'm not aware of it. As a punishment I've worked out an amusing little trick: in the middle of the night I start the sound track. Instead of just standing there with my yellow star and a loving expression on my face, I start the sound track and let him hear a few voices. It's the voices of the mothers that upset him particularly. There were about forty of us in the grave we were forced to dig for ourselves before being machine-gunned, and naturally there were some mothers with their children in the lot. So I play for him, with stark realism—when it comes to art, I'm a stickler for realism—the screams of the Jewish mothers a few seconds before the machine-gun bursts, when they finally understood that their children wouldn't be spared. At a moment like that, a Jewish mother can make a lot of sound, at least a thousand decibels.

You should see my friend Schatzchen bolt up in bed then, his face ash-gray, his eyes bulging. He hates noise.

Excuse my digression. I've told so many Jewish stories at the Shwarze Shikse and other fine places that when I know a good one I simply have to share it with the audience. It's historical with me. No, not hysterical: historical. Same thing.

Schatz throws a quick glance at the report Guth has put on his desk. "Any new developments?"

"Nothing," says Guth. "Not since the land inspector. The coroner now says that he must have been killed a little before the veterinarian. Always in the same manner: a knife in the heart, from the back. I've doubled the patrols."

"We'll have to ask for reinforcements from Lantz."

Schatzchen mops his brow. This crime wave is a desperately serious business for him: his whole career is at stake. If he finds the murderer, he will get a promotion. If not, with all this uproar in the newspapers, he's in for early retirement.

Guth makes an attempt to comfort his superior. He tries to make him see the bright side of things. "It's the crime of the century." Schatz raises his pale eyes. "I've heard that before. People always say that."

He's right. Guth is really going too far. An ignoramus. The crime of the century indeed. What about me, then?

"You'll have to talk to the press," says Guth. "We've got to feed all those big, gaping mouths, or they'll really go after us. 'The negligence and total incompetence of the police . . . the lethargy of the local authorities . . .' I can see the headlines."

"Who cares?" mutters Schatz. "I'm used to it. Every time there's a murder it's always our fault. Everybody knows that. What about the new fingerprints? You had them examined?"

"They're exactly the same as all the others. We've checked them against those of every known sadist, psychotic, and sex deviate in our files. No luck."

"There you are," says Schatz. "Not the slightest clue, not a shadow of a motive . . . and twenty-two corpses. And can you tell me why all the victims have that expression of absolute delight on their faces? You'd think it was the best thing that had ever happened to them in their lousy lives. Guth, I don't even begin to understand any of it. In all my experience I never came across such happy-looking stiffs. Expressions of radiant beatitude! Did you see that veterinarian? He was positively beaming. . . . Total bliss. I've never seen anything more repulsive. The whole business is nerve-racking."

"It's a bit unsettling, in a curious way," admits Guth. "And what with this heat . . ."

True enough, it's hot. Even I've noticed it. Generally speaking, in my present condition—a certain lack of substance, of consistence: we Jews have always been given to abstractions —I'm not at all sensitive to temperature. But since the beginning of this crime wave, I've been experiencing some very odd sensations. Tinglings. Flutterings. Something like barely perceptible caresses. The air is filled with a kind of soft, warm, promising femininity. Even the light becomes a little unreal, it glows intensely, as if it were only there to form a halo around something or somebody. It's no longer a natural light: there's a touch of human skill and genius about it. It's an *artistic* light. You find yourself suddenly thinking of Giotto, of Raphael, of all the Madonnas in the Renaissance frescoes, of all those great accomplishments that owe so much to art and so little to reality. For some time now I've been experiencing a strangely exhilarating impression, as if the whole world were bracing itself for an earthshaking event, for an apotheosis of such sublime beauty that soon there would not be a trace left of human air pollution, not a sign of impurity or imperfection anywhere. *Mazel tov,* as we say in Yiddish, which means: from the bottom of the heart, congratulations. I've always been for the Gioconda, a hundred percent.

"In twenty years of police service," says Schatz, "I've never come across such delight in a corpse. Never. Paradisiacal ex-

11

pressions, that's the only way to describe them. Even the coroner was upset. This is the only thing we have to find out, and I bet it will provide a key to all the murders. *What did those bastards see?* Because they did see something, just before they were killed, and it had to be quite a sight . . . some kind of absolute fulfillment. . . . Those guys looked as if they had been waiting all their lives to get it . . ."

I notice that Hübsch, the clerk, is showing some signs of agitation. The words "quite a sight" and "absolute satisfaction" seem to have a most precise meaning in his mind and a most happy effect on him. I'm amazed and a little shocked. Hübsch looks as if he had been stuffed and preserved in mothballs, but there's little doubt that underneath this appearance here's one of those German romantics. He must be a dreamer, a great sentimentalist, even though it manifests itself in a rather odd way. I wasn't expecting this kind of monumental yearning in an obscure pen-pusher.

"Besides, there was no sign of a struggle," says Guth.

"Right. You'd think they were only too eager to oblige. That they asked nothing better than . . . than *what?* Can you tell me?"

Guth sticks a finger under his collar and twists his neck uneasily. Hot. Very hot. Schatz stares at his subordinate almost threateningly.

"Ecstatic grins . . . Positively beaming while giving up their last . . . Man, I am asking you: what is there on this earth to put a guy in such a state of grace? Can you tell me?"

Guth opens his mouth as if to say something, then apparently thinks better of it and merely looks embarrassed. Hübsch, his fountain pen up in the air, half rises from his chair and stares wildly at a point in space, as if in a trance. His Adam's apple moves spasmodically above his very stiff, starched collar. He swallows hard. His head begins to shake. . . . I'm worried about that boy.

"What could there be so desirable and so enchanting as to make a man go to his death as if it were the luckiest break he'd ever had? . . . What's the matter, Hübsch? You seem all worked up. Do you by any chance have some bright idea on this matter?"

Hübsch sinks back in his chair and cringes. He wipes the tip of his fountain pen in his hair and begins to write assiduously. There are beads of sweat on his forehead. I'm sure he's never had a woman in all his life.

"What about the chemical tests?" asks Schatz. "Maybe they were all drugged. I hear there's this new stuff, LSD. I'm told it can induce heavenly visions. That would explain everything."

Guth is quite firm. "Not a trace of drugs."

"There are some that don't show in a laboratory test. They say you can see God . . . things like that."

"I don't think God's got anything to do with this."

"Anyway, they were in a state of ecstasy," Schatz repeats stubbornly. "There's got to be something mystical about it. Ritual murders?"

"Come now, sir, we're not dealing with Aztecs. Human sacrifices do not take place in Germany."

It's then that Schatz makes a statement that I simply cannot accept, particularly when you consider that it comes from a friend.

"It's the first time in all my experience," he declares solemnly, "that somebody's carrying out mass murders without a motive, without a shadow of a reason. . . ."

That's too much. I can't let him get away with such *hutzpeh*, such gall. The time has come to refresh his memory.

I show myself.

I appear in front of Schatzchen and stare at him, with my big, reproachful eyes.

I'm pleased to note that it shakes him a bit. Let me tell you that I make quite a sight. I'm wearing a long black coat over my Auschwitz-style striped pajamas and, right over the heart, the infamous yellow Star of David, as the regulations required it. My face is very pale, ghastly white, in fact: no matter how courageous you are, when the machine guns are aimed at you and the order *Feuer!* is already on the officer's lips, it does something to you, no use denying that. I'm covered with plaster and chalk from head to toe: coat, nose, hair, everything. We were made to dig our graves among the ruins of an industrial plant in the Forest of Geist. The factory had been destroyed by the Allied Air Force and the idea was to punish us on the spot, symbolically, so to speak. Our corpses were left piled up on top of one another for quite a while, also symbolically. It was there that Schatz, who was the young officer in charge of the execution, picked me up, without realizing it at the time.

I have to mention here a rather interesting point. We were all naked when the shooting began, and I was no exception. You may therefore wonder how it is that I am standing here fully dressed. It's quite simple: Schatz *dressed me.* He has been unable to get rid of me, but his typically German sense of decency and decorum has remained very strong, and though he can't help seeing me, he does at least manage to see me properly dressed. The son of a bitch is a perfect example of rigid middle-class morality.

So here I am, at Police Headquarters, 12 Goethestrasse, staring reproachfully into my friend's eyes. My hair bristles as if my whole head were planted with long, chalk-covered, petrified flashes of lightning: it stood on end in horror and has remained that way, as if it had been graced with this interesting artistic effect for all eternity. I must look like some sort of ghostly Harpo Marx. It wasn't so much fear that made my hair stand up this way: it was the noise. I've always been easily unnerved by noise, and all those mothers with their

14

kids in their arms waiting to be shot made a helluva noise. I don't want to sound anti-Semitic, but nothing screams like a Jewish mother when her kids are being murdered. After all these centuries, they're still unable to adjust. I didn't even have any earplugs on me. I was completely helpless.

2.

A Yiddle
with a Fiddle

My friend Schatz stares at me with a kind of indignant horror: he had never expected to see me in his office. It's the first time I've followed him there. And I can assure you that I didn't miss my entrance. A good sense of timing is essential in the business, as any good comedian will tell you: a second too soon or too late, and you no longer get a laugh. Schatzchen has therefore barely finished saying "It's the first time in all my experience that somebody's carrying out mass murders without a motive, without a shadow of a reason," when I dance in from the wings. At the Shwarze Shikse I always made my entrance like this, dancing in from the wings to a little old Jewish tune played on a fiddle.

The Commissioner freezes, his face becomes ashen, his eyes bulge and he gulps. What's more, he *speaks to me*. He has never yet done this in public. Until now our relationship has been strictly private, very confidential; not even his closest friends are aware of the hidden treasure that Schatz carries within him.

"It's not at all the same thing," he says in a choked voice. "There was a war on. There was an ideology, strong political and philosophical motivations. . . . Besides, I was merely carrying out orders."

I nod approvingly: I know, I understand. I don't want him to give it another thought. I lean over Schatzchen tenderly and remove a speck of dust from his collar. He recoils in terror and I feel a bit hurt. That's no way to treat a buddy.

Inspector Guth and the clerk are watching their chief in stunned silence: neither of them can see me. They are both in their early thirties and you don't learn these things in German schools. They know about me only by hearsay and it's old hat to them anyway.

I take a little clothes brush from my pocket and proceed to dust Schatzchen from head to foot, as if he were a statue. We want him impeccable. Next I spit on his shoulder, where I've just noticed a naughty little bit of fluff and rub off the spot delicately with my sleeve. I stand back a bit, head to one side, and admire my work. He's beautiful. I'm a born do-gooder. But I'm misunderstood. Schatz pushes back his chair with a snarl.

"Enough!" he roars. "I've had enough of this persecution! For twenty years now . . . Leave me alone, damn it!"

I go "okay, okay," with both my hands and dance off whistling the *Horst Wessel Lied*. Tunes from the last war are quite popular in Germany now. New recordings are made of them, old ones are dusted off. Chancellor Erhard went to the United States to ask for nuclear weapons; he came back empty-handed and was removed from office. We're having a quiet little Renaissance here. The new Chancellor Kiesinger had even belonged to the Nazi Party in a burst of youthful enthusiasm and idealism that lasted briefly from 1932 to 1945. Which reminds me that when Professor Herbert Lewin was named head of the Offenbach General Hospital near Frankfurt some years ago, the majority of municipal councilors opposed the appointment on interesting ethical grounds. They gave as their reason that—and I quote—"it is impossible to trust a Jewish doctor and expect him to treat German women impartially, after what happened to the Jews." I clipped this precious little item from the magazine section of the London *Sunday Times*, October 16, 1966, and tacked it on the wall over the john in Schatzchen's bathroom, so that he wouldn't feel safe from me, even in there.

"This is intolerable!" shouts Schatz.

Inspector Guth observes him with a worried eye. Hübsch has shot up from his chair and watches his chief in utter bewilderment. Both are aware that Schatz has been driving himself mercilessly since the murders began and that he drinks too much. But now he seems on the brink of a nervous collapse. By the way, did you know that Eichmann always carried the picture of a little girl in his pocket? Some little thing always eludes you in your striving for perfection.

"Are you talking to me, sir?" says Guth.

"Never mind," mutters Schatz. "It's my——"

I bet he was going to say, "It's my Jew again," but he catches himself.

"It's my spells again," he mumbles.

He grabs the bottle and takes another drink, a thing he has never done before when on duty. I don't like it. I don't like it at all. The bastard is trying to drown me.

"I always get these spells when I'm overworked. But it rarely happens to me in broad daylight and during office hours. . . . Well, never mind. Go tell those 'influential gentlemen' that I can't see them right now. Tell 'em I'm busy, literally besieged by corpses."

I rapidly cross the office in a brisk, businesslike way. Schatzchen's eyes follow me and he brings his fist down hard on the desk.

"It's got to stop!" he bellows. "This persecution's got to stop!"

"All right, I'll tell them," says Guth, who thinks the Commissioner is talking about the two gentlemen who insist on an interview. "But you should really take a little rest, sir. There's no point in killing yourself."

"I've always done my duty right to the very end," says Schatz.

That's true enough and I feel that some mark of appreciation is due him. I appear instantly with a little bunch of forget-me-nots in my hand and put them in the glass on Schatzchen's desk. I'm full of these delicate attentions. But the Commissioner merely looks like an enraged bull. He lowers his head and stares at the flowers with bloodshot eyes, as if he were going to charge. Then he begins to pound the desk again.

"Take those flowers away!" he bellows in a drunken voice.

Inspector Guth and Hübsch exchange surprised glances.

"What flowers?" asks Guth. "There are no flowers . . ."

Schatz takes a deep breath, but I'm not at all sure it does him any good. I'm part of it. It's a strictly chemical process, nothing supernatural about it. Atoms. Particles. A whiff and a sniff of something or other. Let me put it this way: I'm here to stay.

"Wouldn't you like to lie down for a moment?" asks Guth.

Guth is young. Thirty-one, thirty-two. Tall, blond, strong, a Nordic type that always makes a good impression at the Olympics. He's a German of the new generation: for them I don't mean a thing. They will even tell you: "There are no more Jews in Germany." They believe it, too. They inhale and exhale in blissful ignorance. They are not even anti-Semitic, and when they are a bit, it's merely out of respect for their elders.

"It's worse when I lie down," says Schatz in a dull voice. "The moment I do, that bastard gets on my chest. . . ."

He corrects himself. "I mean, I've got a weight on my chest, an oppression." Guth knows all about it. "Metabolism," he says. "Metabolism, that's the thing. You've got to eliminate.

When you don't, it piles up inside you and you're in trouble. You've got to eliminate, any doctor'll tell you that."

I nod. He couldn't have put it better.

I am very careful now to keep discreetly in the shadows, as I don't want Schatzchen to become used to this new development in our relationship, which is my appearance in his office. I therefore give him what the Gestapo used to call a moment of "psychological relief." In the comedy business this is known as "nursing the public." Schatzchen is my only and in all probability my last audience and it's essential not to saturate your audience. You mustn't try to keep the public laughing all the time. As any entertainer will tell you, if the jokes come too close together, they lose their impact. The audience becomes saturated. To get another laugh you have to give them that moment of "psychological relief" the Gestapo knew so well. In comedy, as I told you before, timing is the thing.

I therefore make myself as inconspicuous as I can and I realize that I've done the right thing. Schatz can no longer see me and the feeling of relief is such that he proceeds to make a confession.

"Guth, I've got *tsuris*," he says.

I'm pleased. I like to hear my friend Schatz speak Yiddish. It's a tribute to which I'm particularly sensitive.

"Excuse me?" says Guth.

Schatz turns red in the face. I don't at all see why he should feel ashamed. There's no harm in taking foreign language lessons, even in the middle of the night.

"I'm in trouble. Listen, Guth, you're a friend. I'm going to tell you something. You probably won't understand. You're too young, your generation has been spared that. . . . It's a Jew."

"A Jew?"

"Yes. A particularly tenacious and hostile one, with a chip

on his shoulder and who won't let me alone. He's of the kind who can't forgive . . . the *exterminated* kind. They're the toughest ones. They have no heart."

I shrug. Exterminated, that's easier said than done. There are some dead who never die. I would even say that the more you kill them the more they are there. Take Germany. Today it's a country entirely inhabited by Jews. Of course, you can't see them, they don't have any physical presence, but . . . how shall I put it? They make themselves *felt*. Walk around in German cities, as well as in Warsaw and other places rich in German history, and you feel a strange, heavy, Jewish presence in the air. It's a terrible thing we have done to them and it causes a lot of resentment and anti-Semitism. They won't be able to get rid of us unless they destroy themselves, God forbid.

"What do you mean, sir? What Jew?"

"I knew you wouldn't understand," Schatz says gloomily. "I've got a Jew on my back, that's what. Of course, it's only a hallucination—I am perfectly aware of that—but knowing it doesn't help a bit. It's awful."

"Have you seen a doctor?"

"What do you think? This has been going on for twenty-four years. I've seen piles and piles and piles . . ."

He stops dead. I've made a little sign to him from the shadows and he has seen me. He assumes a dignified air.

"Piles of *doctors*, I mean. But they haven't done a thing. If you ask me, they don't want to get involved again. When I tell them I'm being driven nuts by a Jewish parasite who keeps me awake at night and undermines my physical and moral fiber, they act embarrassed. They've heard that before, you understand. Remember, they're German doctors, and they don't want to have anything to do with it. Suppose they manage to rid me of my Jew, they're afraid they'll be accused of genocide again. I've thought of going to Israel for treatment—we do have a cultural agreement with them—but it's rather delicate. After all, you can't ask an Israeli doctor to suppress a Jew just to make a German feel better. I don't even try anymore."

Guth seems interested, which pleases me. I can do with a larger audience.

"Is it always the same guy?"

"Always."

"Did you . . . had you . . . well, I mean . . . did you know him personally?"

"No, I didn't know him and there was nothing personal about this, it was a general policy. But I couldn't help noticing him because when I was about to shout *'Feuer!'* . . . I had my orders, you understand, I was a soldier and I had to carry them out, the honor of the German Army was at stake, our whole tradition of discipline and sense of duty. . . . In short, when I was about to give the order, he surprised me, because he didn't behave like the others. There were about forty of them, men, women, children. . . . Hitler has done terrible things to us. They were all waiting at the bottom of the hole we made them dig. They didn't seem to believe what was happening at first, then the mothers in the group began to scream. . . . But nobody made any special attempt to do anything about it—not that they could've, mind you. For once, even the Jews had reached the end of their tricks. All except one. He wasn't like the others. *He fought back."*

"Fought back? With what? I thought the Jews had no weapons."

"No weapons, no weapons . . . This one seemed to think he had one left. We had made them undress to save the clothing, the German economy was at its lowest ebb. They were all stark naked and just as I was about to shout *'Feuer!'* this son of a bitch turned his back to the firing squad, bent over and . . ."

I have often wondered what it was that made me show him my bare ass at such a tragic moment. I suppose it was my artistic temperament, a last sudden flash of inspiration. Or was it a kind of prophecy, a premonition, almost as if I had foreseen that the Jews would one day be accused of having gone to their death like sheep, without fighting back? The only weapon we had was our bare ass, so I used mine.

"I was so shocked at such a lack of dignity in the face of death that I hesitated a second or two before shouting '*Feuer!*' and the son of a bitch even managed to shout '*Kush mir in tokhes*' before he fell. . . ."

There have undoubtedly been more worthy and noble last words in history than "Kiss my ass," but I have never made any claim to greatness and, besides, I'm quite pleased with my effort and only hope that my message will go down to posterity and that I will have thus contributed a little something to our spiritual heritage. I do not wish to sound bitter, but I do believe that six million Jews left without any help at all by the civilized world could not address the latter a more heartfelt and befitting message than "Kiss my ass," or that the civilized world deserved anything more noble and dignified. Anyone who thinks otherwise should have his conscience examined.

I didn't know at the time that by fighting back I would impress Schatz so deeply, cause him some kind of traumatic shock and stay with him forever, thus achieving a sort of immortality. All I wanted was to express myself. But Schatzchen never got over it. The whole thing became intensely personal to him. As he stood there with the order *"Feuer!"* stuck in his throat, looking me in the eye—if I may be permitted to sound a bit risqué, though as a rule I avoid off-color jokes in my act—something happened to him. He still managed to give the order, as befits an officer, but a beautiful relationship was already born. He made it even deeper by taking the trouble

23

to find out who I was, going through my papers and diaries, trying to learn as much as he could about the arrogant and defiant Jew who fought back.

I don't know what happened to the others in my group, if any of them were picked up by some young soldiers in the firing squad. Who can tell? For all I know, there may be a Jew sitting right now at the Council table of the Bonn Government, unnoticed, undetected, his presence and weight known only to his distinguished carrier.

"Can you imagine?" mutters Schatz. *"Kush mir in tokhes!"* Real *hutzpeh!"*

There is a moment of silence.

"I didn't know you spoke Yiddish," says Guth.

The Commissioner seems thunderstruck. "Did I speak Yiddish?"

"That's what it sounded like to me."

"Gott in Himmler!" says Schatz.

I'm hurt. Why should he be so upset? Considering all the time we've spent together it's the most natural thing in the world that I should have taught him a thing or two.

"He's at it again," mutters Schatz. "You're right, Guth. He does make me talk Yiddish, often in the middle of the night. . . ."

True enough. I give him a few lessons now and then. So what? What's wrong with a bit of learning? Besides, Schatz-chen snores. Sometimes I even suspect that he's having a beautiful dream. Escapism, I call it. Flight from reality. So I wake him up and we have a little Yiddish lesson. It's very enriching. We have a beautiful literature. Soon Schatzchen will be able to read Sholom Aleichem in the original. Where's the harm?

I begin to notice that Inspector Guth and Hübsch watch their superior warily and that they exchange meaningful glances from time to time. I must admit that they have some reason to worry. Schatzchen has half risen from his chair and leans forward over his desk, staring at me fixedly, muttering and shaking his fist. Careful now. If I ride him too hard, he will go completely out of his mind and what will become of me then? I can't afford to lose him. Twenty years of beautiful hospitality. So, I make myself invisible again.

"This is none of my business, of course," says Guth, "but you ought to take a tranquilizer, Chief."

"The son of a bitch doesn't like that," says Schatz.

Now, that's a lie. He can stuff himself with tranquilizers for all I care. They have no effect on history. No bloody pill can kick me out of his subconscious. I'm telling you: I'm there to stay.

For generations, the defenders of a racially pure Germany have called us Jews "the enemy within," and now at last they've succeeded in getting us truly inside them. I suppose this is what Jung calls the "collective subconscious." Not one Jew I know enjoys being there—the place stinks to heaven, just like any other subconscious—but it will take many a generation before they get rid of us.

"I often catch myself using words in that horrible jargon," mutters Schatz. "In the end, I had to buy myself a Yiddish dictionary, so as to understand myself. A few key words. . . . *Rakhmones* . . . that means pity. I must have heard it a million times in Poland. *Gevalt,* help. *Hutzpeh,* cheek. And the other night . . . can you imagine that? I woke up singing."

Inspector Guth smiles pleasantly. "There's nothing wrong with that," he says.

"It depends," Schatz grumbles angrily. "You know what that *ganif* made me sing? *El molorakhmin.* It's their funeral chant for the dead. . . . He woke me up a little after midnight —I later realized that it was the anniversary of the rising of the Warsaw ghetto—and before I knew it he had me singing at the top of my voice the Hebrew chant for the dead. . . . He

25

was sitting on my bed, his arms crossed, listening, with a terrifying, mad gleam in his eyes. After that, he made me sing *Yiddishe Mamme*. The son of a bitch has no tact whatsoever. After all, there were mothers and children among those innocent victims of Hitler. Then, just as the night was ending, he jumped from the bed, forced me onto my knees, and made me recite the *Kaddish*, their prayer for the dead. In my own house, in a nice German neighborhood. Real *hutzpeh*, I call it. *Tfou, tfou, tfou.*"

Inspector Guth takes a step back and exchanges a significant glance with the secretary. "He's gone stark, raving mad," that's what the glance means, if I interpret it correctly, and Hübsch nods quickly, hovering over his files like a kind of bland, paper-fed vulture.

"On your knees?" repeats Guth. "He made you recite the *Kaddish* on your knees? That's odd. I thought Jews didn't go down on their knees to pray."

Schatz looks around suspiciously and lowers his voice. *"We made them kneel,"* he mutters, in a confidential tone. . . . "We always made them kneel before shooting, as soon as they had finished digging."

"I see," says Guth, in a slightly shaken voice, and I must say to his credit that the young German's face suddenly turns ashen.

3.

On a Point
of
History

Here I wish to make a statement. In my group, no one went down on his knees. I am aware that posthumous evidence is considered suspect, but there's a survivor, who simply lost a leg in the incident, Albert Katz, of Number 3 Bracka Street, Cracow, and he can bear witness to this. Next to him, on my right, there was a whole family, the Katzenelenbogens, then Jakob Tennenbaum, the journalist, the engineer Gedanke, and a very pretty girl of fourteen, Tsatsa Sardinenfish.

These names surely seem ridiculous to you and they have made Eastern European Jewry a laughingstock for generations. There are still some people who feel that Hitler has merely wiped out a lot of ludicrous names.

Let me explain this point of history to you. When we came to Germany, Poland, and Russia, we called ourselves "son of Aaron," "son of Isaac," "son of Abraham." We were still the people of the Bible. And the local authorities had lots of fun inventing witty names for us. *Goldkopf,* goldenhead. *Briskin,* the circumcized one. *Gedanke,* many thanks. *Sutchkin,* little son of a bitch. Et cetera. There's nothing like a

27

good laugh. Montaigne, the French thinker, wrote that "laughter is a deeply human trait." He was right.

But let's get back to my friend Schatz. He's still trying to justify himself, to set that record straight.

"It's all the Pope's fault," he says. "There's a wonderful play by a very bright young man called Hochhuth on this subject. If Pope Pius XII had said one word, we would have had a good excuse not to kill the Jews. That's all we were waiting for: an excuse not to kill them. With my own hands, I would not have killed them! But no, the Pope didn't stretch out a helping hand to us. So we had no excuse not to kill them. And now they have taken over, Guth. They have occupied us; Germany today is a country occupied by five million Jews. . . . "

"Six million."

"Five and a half . . . All right, let's make it six, it doesn't matter. And anyway I am concerned with only one of them. You know what he did last week? I was relaxing in front of the fire, reading the *Diary of Anne Frank*, and there he was again suddenly, out of nowhere, coming up with a new idea. He had me promise to eat kosher till the end of my life."

That's a bloody lie. I made no such demands. But when you share another person's life, it's only normal that the other party acquires some of your own habits and tastes. If Schatz wishes to eat kosher, that's strictly his business. He even cooks himself some of our traditional little dishes, on Friday night, cholent, gefilte fish, tsimis. What's wrong with that? I always get hungry in the evening.

"In my opinion, sir," says Guth, "you think too much about these things. You ought to spend a little time in an Arab country to disintoxicate yourself."

Schatz sighs heavily and fingers the reports on his desk. "With all those murders on my hands, I can't allow myself

28

to take a holiday, Guth, we've got to solve this case. And we have to do it damn fast, before the assassin strikes again."

"If you do, sir, you'll be the most famous man in Germany. You'll have your picture in all the papers."

Schatz looks apprehensive, but he is wrong to worry about it. He has changed so much in the last twenty years that no one would recognize him.

"What am I to tell Baron von Pritwitz and Count zu Zahn?" asks Guth. "They say you have been instructed by phone from Chancellor Kiesinger's office to receive them immediately."

"Tell them that I am terribly sorry, but I have an important case on my hands and . . ."

I am pleased. I like to be recognized as an "important case." I appear before Schatzchen, grab his hand and shake it. Then I sit down on his desk, clasp my hands round my knees and nonchalantly swing one foot, looking at my friend lovingly, and whistling: *Bei mir bist du sheyn*. Schatz assumes a dignified air and pretends he hasn't seen me.

Guth leaves the office. The Commissioner has turned himself into a statue of indignant gravity, like a man in the throes of delirium tremens who sees a rat on his knee but knows it's a mere hallucination. I whistle softly. Hübsch, his nose buried in papers, writes assiduously, from time to time throwing a quick, frightened glance toward his superior. Schatz takes up the glass from the desk and fills it. He hesitates a moment, then pushes the glass toward me. I shake my head in stern refusal. He sighs and drinks it himself. He taps the table casually with his fingertips, opens a drawer and takes out a packet of *matzos,* takes one and presents it to me. I refuse again. My friend sighs and puts the packet back in the drawer. Then he observes that Hübsch has risen from his chair and is watching him, his mouth gaping, with an air of total, terrified imbicility. The Commissioner's face turns red. I understand how he feels. There's nothing more vexing than to be caught by a subordinate during a tender exchange with a person dear to your heart. Schatz explodes.

"What is it now, Hübsch? Is anything wrong?"

The clerk vanishes behind his files.

Schatz drinks gloomily. I sometimes get the impression that he has lost his sense of humor. I seem unable to make him laugh. It makes me feel a failure. You know how it is with us comedians; we've got to get a laugh. We thrive on laughter. Fortunately, there's still a good audience in Germany for Jewish comics. If you don't believe me, all you have to do is to open the London *Sunday Times* color supplement of October 16, 1966. We now have a new rabbi in Berlin, Rabbi David Weïz. Well, he confided to the English newspaper that what surprises and saddens him is—and here I quote: "The way the Berliners point and laugh at him when he comes out of the synagogue and all the way home." That Frenchman, Montaigne, was right. Laughter is a deeply human characteristic.

The telephone buzzes and Schatz answers it.

"Yes, sir . . . The Chancellor himself? I see . . . No, unfortunately, not a clue, not for the moment. We have questioned over three hundred people. All the roads leading to the Forest of Geist are guarded and we have forbidden access to the woods until further notice. Still, a few sensation seekers manage to get through. . . . Morbid curiosity! I begin to have the feeling that some people simply long to get murdered. . . . In my opinion, sir, it's some kind of organization . . . perhaps a ritual sect of a new kind. . . . I know, sir, but I cannot prevent the world press from insulting us. They're always bringing up the Düsseldorf vampire. You would think they could have come up with something more recent. . . . "

More recent? Your very humble servant. I wave gaily, and Schatzchen gives me a crushing look.

"Yes, sir, I will see these two gentlemen at once. I had not been told they were recommended by the Chancellor himself. I'll also talk to the press. Yes, sir, immediately. I fully realize the importance of the world's public opinion and of the new German image. Thank you, sir."

He hangs up and mumbles an obscenity. He didn't sleep a wink last night—we were having a little history lesson—and he needs to pass his nerves on to someone. If I show myself again, he is quite capable of throwing an inkpot at my head. He's a Lutheran, and these people have a horror of demons.

"Hübsch!"

"*Jawohl!*"

The clerk jumps up and waits.

"How many times do I have to tell you not to wipe your pen in your hair? Repulsive habit. You ought to consult a psychiatrist."

"*Jawohl!*"

The Commissioner leaves the office, Hübsch remains standing for a moment, contemplating his pen. He wipes it sadly in his hair and sits down again.

I experience a familiar feeling of emptiness, a loss of identity and of memory, as I do every time Schatz manages to overcome my presence, and I sink slowly, deeper and deeper, into a darkness full of vaguely stirring, shapeless and nameless horrors, a stinking and frightening pit which has been my prison for more than twenty-three years now.

The subsconscious of a former Waffen SS, I would not wish that upon my best friend.

I hate the place: you never know whom you might meet there. Would you believe me? The other night, I ran smack into something that at first I took for a fabrication of a sick mind: a new German army, with all its panzers back on their feet again, atomic artillery, *Luftwaffe,* and young eager generals. *Tfou, tfou, tfou.*

The German subconscious, I would not wish that upon my best friend.

4.

The Elite

I am thus lost in somber thoughts, wandering among our classics, when the door opens and a gentleman in grand attire —gray bowler hat, exquisite gloves, Prince of Wales check suit, pearl pin in a gray silk tie, walking stick, spats, Goethe, Chamisso, Beethoven, Schopenhauer—walks in, in a state of anguished agitation. His blue, romantic eyes have the hurt, uncomprehending expression of a man awakened from a beautiful dream by a ghastly reality. He is followed by a tall, thin, elegant individual wearing gray tweeds, the most striking thing about whom is his nose: it is one of those prominent, hooked noses that are called either aristocratic or Jewish, which have been greatly admired in the Bourbon dynasty since Louis XIV, but which have caused us nothing but trouble. This man has, no doubt about it, a fine, distinguished presence, with a parting in the middle. I am talking about his hair—and he would make me think of Alfred Krupp, if I were capable of thinking about such a thing.

The two gentlemen make a good impression on me. There is nobility in the air, quality, good manners, delicacy, tradition, *savoir-faire*. I run over to them and sniff. They smell good. Eau de Cologne, English tobacco, excellent leather. They don't smell at all of rotting corpses and gas chambers. Anyhow, there are no more war criminals: they have all taken up other jobs. I permit myself to finger delicately the material of which their suits are made: great stuff, at least fifteen marks a yard and, believe me, sir, at that price I lose money. I know what I am talking about: my father, Jakob Cohn, was a tailor in Lodz. I have several generations of tailors behind me. My father loved a well-cut suit, quality goods, silk linings; he was always well-dressed himself, except at the time of his execution: they were all stripped naked. Let me make one point clear: it was not cruelty. The Germans were short of everything at the end of the war and they merely wanted to recover the clothing intact, without bullet holes.

I often get the impression that the Mona Lisa's smile is pure vandalism.

Hübsch gets up and greets the two men respectfully. I don't care much for that man. There is something eternal and sinister about him, which dimly implies History. He is the man of well-kept registers and scrupulous records. Ever since the first massacre this strange creature has tiptoed through the march of History, respectful, meticulous, attentive, a goose quill or a scribe's tablet in his hand, noting that on such and such a day, in such and such a place, the economy of the tribe, of the nation, or of the state has been enriched by so many gold bridges, so many pairs of children's shoes, so many tons of human hair. When Hitler ordered the massacre of Gypsies, it is said that many of the men killed their wives and families themselves, thereby robbing the SS of the only satisfaction they could have derived from contact with an inferior race. Gypsies are robbers, we all know that.

"The Commissioner will be here in a second," says Hübsch.

He goes behind his desk and buries himself in his papers again. All that can be seen of him is his pen, scratching away. The idea occurs to me that this meticulous bureaucrat is preparing records for the Day of Judgment. I have to admit that I have a certain leaning toward the fantastic, under the influence of good German literature, no doubt, the Brothers Grimm, Chamisso. . . . Do you know the story by Chamisso: The man who could never lose his shadow, no matter how hard he tried? That's absolutely Schatzchen and me.

As for the Last Judgment, I keep forgetting that it has already taken place, that sentence has been passed and carried out, and that is how, as punishment, man was created.

It is a mistake to say that we the Jews believe in a severe, merciless God. We know that God can be very human; He even has His moments of absentmindedness, just like everyone else: sometimes He forgets a man, and that makes one happy life.

I now recognize the two distinguished gentlemen who are waiting for Schatz. I have seen their pictures in the Society column of the *Zeitung*. They have amassed considerable fortunes since what is known as the "German miracle," and they spend this money generously: they build museums, patronize the arts, finance symphony orchestras, and offer their Dürers and their Rembrandts to the City's Hall of Culture. I must admit that right now beauty is greatly encouraged all over the world. In the U.S.A. there is such an overflow of art treasures, music, and books that you could rape your grandmother there, no one would notice.

I have no reservations about our culture vultures. If Christ —peace to His ashes—were to rise again and look at all the splendors and beauty of the Renaissance crucifixions, He would be indignant, insulted in every drop of His blood. It has always appeared to me that to make beauty out of His agony, to use His martyrdom to procure delight, is not very Christian. I think the popes ought to have looked into it. In my humble opinion, the Church should have forbidden the Renaissance masters to capitalize on the Crucifixion and should have left the artistic exploitation and profiteering of the Fra Filippo Lippi and Giotto type to us unworthy Jews, like the practice of usury.

The shorter of the two gentlemen, the one whose suit is made of cloth at fifteen marks the yard, seems terribly upset. His pink, rather babyish face shows signs of extreme inner stress, his little gray moustache twitches nervously, and he can't keep still: even his indignant, dismayed blue eyes keep rolling around and around in anguish.

"Believe me, Count, no one is more appalled by the prospect of a scandal than I am, but I have no choice left. I have to tell the police. If anything should happen to her, I would never forgive myself. And with all those horrors one reads in the papers . . . These ghastly murders . . . I fear the worst."

"My dear Baron, you are not the first husband whose wife has run off with the gamekeeper."

"My dear Count, I am not claiming the place of honor. There is no longer any question of my pride. It is quite simple, a question of love. Of a very great, very beautiful love."

"That's exactly what I was saying, when referring to the gamekeeper."

The Baron glares at the Count. The Count glares at the Baron.

"Of *my* love."

"Of love in general," barks the Count.

They keep glaring at each other. I begin to feel that here we have what is known as a "situation."

"This conversation, my dear Count, is wholly out of place. I am too unhappy."

"We all are."

The two noblemen glare at each other and start walking round and round again. I have to say this: I have a great sympathy for betrayed husbands. I have drawn some of my best comic effects from them. You have only to mention the word "cuckold" and the audience roars with laughter. Wounded pride is our oldest and surest source of comedy. You probably all remember a certain snapshot of a Hasidic Jew, one of those Jews who look so funny with their beards and long locks of hair, *peyes,* falling on their cheeks, their hats and their long, black caftans? A soldier is posing in this famous photograph: he is laughing for posterity, while pulling the Hasidic Jew by the beard. And what do you think the Hasidic Jew is doing while being pulled by the beard, standing there all alone among the laughing, humorous German soldiers? *He is laughing too.*

As Montaigne so rightly said, laughter is a deeply human characteristic.

"I am afraid she may have fallen victim to this sadist everybody is talking about. Can you imagine her lovely, pure body sprawled in the woods . . . God!"

"The gamekeeper will protect her. After all, it is his job."

"I no longer trust him."

"You've trusted him with your game for five years . . ."

The Baron stops and glares at him. The Count fixes his eyeglass under his brow and glares back. Truly there will always be something screamingly funny about the dignified and noble attitude of Man facing the bitter truth about himself.

Remember the burst of laughter which greeted Danton's famous last words on the guillotine? "Show my head to the people, it is well worth it!" I don't really know why the sight of a cuckold's horns above an inspired brow should provoke such hilarity. A feeling of brotherhood, the reassurance of knowing that one is not alone in one's predicament?

5.

The Murders
of the
Forest of Geist

I am thus engaged in lofty meditation, when the door opens and in walks my friend Schatzchen. I have settled comfortably in his chair, but he is so harassed by his other problems that he fails to notice me, he sits on me, both literally and figuratively. I have temporarily ceased to exist for him. Work is the best of therapies.

I must say that in the last few days there has been a real howl of protest and indignation from the press. The police are being accused of incompetence, passivity, negligence, and lack of method. One has to admit that twenty-two murders in eight days are, after all, quite a lot, even for a big country like Germany. The whole of the civilized world is aghast and the press is talking of nothing else. All this falls squarely on Schatzchen's shoulders, as the Forest of Geist and its surroundings, where all the murders occurred, are his responsibility. No wonder he is preoccupied: his career is at stake.

"Good morning, *meine Herren*. What can I do for you?"

Introductions. Politeness. Bows.

"Baron von Pritwitz."

"Count zu Zahn."

"Chief Commissioner Schatz."

"Genghis Cohn."

The Commissioner freezes, then decides to ignore me. Okay. Okay. If he doesn't want me to make new friends, I shall not press myself upon them. The two aristocrats are, of course, a thousand miles away from suspecting my existence. They are above that sort of thing. They had nothing to do with it. Their hands are clean. At the time it happened, they were in Paris, visiting the Louvre.

"Please be seated. Sorry to have kept you waiting. The gutter press . . . All these murders are a godsend for them. What can I do for you?"

The Baron caresses his brow with a very white, admirably cared-for hand. I notice a beautiful ring, a ruby, a family jewel, no doubt. It's worth twenty thousand dollars, give or take a dime. I say that only out of respect for the public: I do not want to upset your habits. I like to conform to the idea you have of a ghetto Jew. For centuries you've been forcing us to conform to the traditional caricature of a greedy Jew your race has drawn of ours, and the first duty of a comedian is to please his audience.

"But I must ask you to be brief. I have twenty-two unsolved murders on my hands and——"

"That's precisely what brought us here," the Baron says. "I am desperately worried about my wife. As you probably know, my family castle is right in the middle of the Forest of Geist and . . . "

He takes a handkerchief out of his pocket and wipes his brow. He cannot speak. The Count takes over from him.

"May I ask if all the victims have been identified?"

"Those who have been found, yes."

The Count takes a photograph out of his pocket and puts it on the desk. The Commissioner takes it. He looks at it a long time. There is an expression of sadness on his face, almost of longing. I have always suspected that there is a German romantic buried in him.

"She is very beautiful. Who is she?"

The Baron sighs. "My wife."

"Congratulations."

"She has disappeared."

"Ah. Well, in any case, I can reassure you on one point. She is not among the victims."

"Are you sure?"

"Certain. It would be too lucky if, for once in my profession, I found a body as beautiful as that. . . . However, all the victims are men, without exception. The murderer, apparently, never touches women. There is another aspect common to all these murders. All the dead have an expression of absolute bliss on their faces . . . a happy expression of total fulfillment . . . "

Something very odd is happening to Hübsch. He is trying to control himself, but it is getting out of hand, quite obviously. However, I'm not going to describe it. In my life, I've already had enough trouble with the censor. They called my repertoire blue and "risqué," and I don't want anyone to start talking again about the "decadent Jewish art," which "threatens our moral fiber and aims at undermining our culture and its values." I don't want them to bring forth Chagall, Soutine, Modigliani, as a proof of our "destructive Yiddish expressionism." I have absolutely no wish to undermine your society. You can have it. You deserve it a hundred percent. *Mazel tov.*

All I shall say is that the word "happiness" appears to have a most precise meaning for Hübsch: he seems to know exactly what it looks like. He has half risen from his chair, holding his fountain pen in the air, and he is staring at a point in space as if the Commissioner's words "absolute bliss" and "total fulfillment" have brought forth a vision, the nature of which I refuse to describe. *Tfou, tfou, tfou.*

" . . . An expression of delight, of rapture . . . One would think that all the victims had died in a state of ecstasy!"

At the word "ecstasy," Hübsch stiffens all over, his pince-nez shines with fanatical yearning, with *Seehnsucht,* as the German romantics call it, a boundless aspiration, and I make sure that my yellow star is in its proper place, so that if it starts again I am in order.

This being said, I don't believe in the revival of Nazism in Germany. They'll find something else.

"There can be no doubt that all these men went to their death happily, even eagerly, as if they were reaching their goal, as if their hand was getting hold at last of something that had always eluded them. The supreme fruit . . . The *absolute.* I shall put it like this: to the best of my knowledge, no one has ever seen such an expression of fulfillment, of achievement, on a dead man's face. One begins to wonder what they saw there, those bas— Excuse me."

A heavy silence, full of *Seehnsucht, Weltschmerz,* and nostalgia settles over the Police Station of Licht, Number 12 Goethestrasse.

6.

The Mystery Deepens

I don't know if this is psychosomatic with me, or some kind of optical effect, but for the last few minutes everything around me glows with a sort of noble and slightly unreal light. This impression is so strong that when Corporal Klepke walks in with the last autopsy report, there's an air of a masterpiece about him, as if the features of his otherwise ordinary face had just emerged from under the brush of a new Dürer. The ghastly idea flashes through my mind that here is another Renaissance in the making and that soon all that will be left of the century's crimes will be magnificent works of art, of which Germany and all humanity will be immensely proud. With a little bit of luck and genius even six million gassed Jews will become a major contribution to Culture.

As a rule, Schatzchen is not given to confiding in strangers. But he is obviously not averse to showing a bit of superior insight, to making a good impression on such distinguished visitors. Besides, this is his case, his opportunity for promotion, public acclaim, and celebrity. The mystery of all these good German *Bürgers* who went to their doom as if to a fiesta haunts him day and night.

"I am beginning to believe, *meine Herren,* that it was death itself that had some special attraction for these men, hence the blissful grins on all their faces. Let me put it this way: it was death of a quite different quality, a new, exalting, highly satisfying experience . . . not at all the usual, vulgar thing."

The Baron shows no interest, but his companion approves and offers his own theory.

"It may well be," says the Count, "that our scientists have invented a new death, worthy at last of our German genius. A death that would have its own Titians, Michelangelos, Leonardos . . . a true perfection, a death worth living for . . . something that our *Kultur* has been groping for since the *Niebelungen*. . . . By the way, *meine Herren,* did you know that with a certain type of shrimp sexual climax lasts twenty-four hours?"

Hübsch almost jumps out of his skin. A romantic. The Commissioner himself is deeply impressed.

"Now, *meine Herren,* please!" the Baron protests. "My wife is in mortal danger and you are discussing philosophy!"

Schatz descends to earth again, after this brief glimpse of the absolute. "You say she has disappeared?"

"Well, that is, she's gone off with . . . with"—he almost chokes—"with my gamekeeper."

The Commissioner opens his mouth to say, no doubt, something tactfully appropriate. This is my opportunity.

"Haven't you got a chauffeur?"

"Certainly, but I don't see——"

"Usually, in high society, it's the chauffeur . . ."

The Baron turns livid. The Count is outraged.

"Sir, you are speaking of Baroness von Pritwitz!"

Schatz is horror-struck. If there's one thing he hates it is when I begin to play ventriloquist with him, using him as a dummy. It was part of my act in the Shwarze Shikse days, and I often enjoy going through my old music-hall routine with my partner.

The Count fixes the monocle again in his eye and stares at Schatz. "He's drunk," he says scornfully.

43

True enough. In fact, Schatz is so drunk that even I begin to experience a certain loss of identity. There are moments when I begin to doubt my own existence. Worse than that: I suddenly become convinced that I am Schatz, Hans Helmut Schatz a former storm trooper and *Judenfresser tfou, tfou, tfou.* As you can see, I'm a bit of a neurotic.

Schatz, obviously, begins to feel that he has nothing more to lose and that the best form of defense is attack.

"*Meine Herren,* don't you read the papers? Bodies everywhere, fear, people shutting themselves in their houses, the press attacking the police with venom, and you wish me to deal with such a strictly personal matter as a runaway wife? I have twenty-two corpses to investigate! All with a radiantly happy expression on their faces and all with their pants off!"

"With their pants off?"

"Yes," Schatz growls. "Bare-assed and with happy smiles."

"Smiles? What do you mean, smiles? Where?"

"Decent women no longer dare to leave their homes."

"But I thought the murderers only attacked men?"

"Decent women don't dare to go out, because of the offensive sight. Twenty-two grinning, bare-assed corpses, that's what I have on my hands. I haven't slept in three nights. I keep seeing their beaming mugs. . . . What did they see, the bastards? What gave them such an expression of sheer delight? Who? What? How? A knife in the back and yet, one would think they had died of utter joy. *What have they seen?*" He thumps the table with his fist.

"*A new Fuehrer?*"

Schatz glares at the two men suspiciously. "Who said that?"

He did. I am a real pro.

Schatz grabs the telephone. "Kuhn? Listen, will you find out if the victims aren't Jewish, by any chance. . . . What do you mean, why? *If all the murdered men should be Jews, then at least we would have a motive!*"

44

Sherlock Holmes, I'm telling you. Sherlock Holmes! That's what Schatzchen is. I'm very proud of him.

He has barely put the phone down when it rings again.

"Yes, good morning, Doctor. . . . I know that. I know perfectly well that they were all subjected to odious violence . . . a knife in the back. *What?* What did you say? The absolute? The old German craving for the absolute? Not the big absolute? The *little* one? What little absolute? Are you sure? Struck during the act, all of them. In full triumph? In full apotheosis? The most beautiful fate, the most inspiring death? Listen, Doctor, everyone knows that you are a true patriot, but try to keep calm. . . . Doctor! DOCTOR!"

He hangs up very quickly, pulls out his handkerchief, and wipes his fingers. "The swine! Into the telephone! Well, gentlemen, we're dealing with the biggest outbreak of sexual crimes since paradise!"

The Commissioner gets up, takes a walk around the office, then sits down again.

"To sum up: no trace of struggle, of resistance. In each case, the trousers were carefully folded, which clearly indicates that all the victims were willing, even eager to oblige. In my opinion, the murderer employs a beautiful, an irresistibly beautiful woman as bait, and strikes the victim in the back while he is busy elsewhere . . ."

"What do you mean, elsewhere?"

The Count is bewildered.

The bureaucrat Hübsch seems to have reached bursting point. He's standing very erect, his eyes bulging, and he looks as though he sees a vision. His moustache quivers under his fevered breath. I don't like what's going on here. I don't like it a bit. Afterwards, they'll say it's a typical example of degenerate, morbid, Jewish art.

"But the incentive? The motive?"

"Perhaps a cuckolded husband," the Count suggests. "He

45

surprised his wife in the arms of a lover and killed him . . ."

"Twenty-two lovers in a week?"

The Count thinks this over.

"Well, maybe she belonged to a circus."

The Commissioner gives him a murderous look. "Any other bright suggestions?"

"I don't know. But it seems to me that when you begin to find corpses by the dozen, there is surely a good explanation. It can't be anything low and ordinary. There's got to be an ideal behind it, a profound faith, a creed, an ideology, a pure, disinterested motive. Some kind of vision, like Mao's, Hitler's, or Stalin's. You say all the victims look delighted. They probably took off their pants and offered themselves freely. A willing sacrifice, on the altar of a great cause."

Schatz grabs the bottle again. "Rotten," he mutters. "All completely rotten. A diabolical, obscene art. . . . I can feel a Jewish presence, pitiless, full of hate, unable to undo what has been done to them, but trampling on our faces . . . twisting, turning . . . Gentlemen, *they are back!* Germany's an occupied country! This whole situation smacks once more of decadent, Jewish expressionistic presence! Chagall! Soutine! They're at our throats again!"

Once more the Baron looks for sympathy. "Commissioner, I quite understand that you are busy, but all the same, I am formally asking you to help me find my wife. It is now eight days since she disappeared——"

"Eight days? What is he like, this gamekeeper of yours?"

"Florian? Perfectly efficient and very meticulous in his work."

"I see."

The Commissioner studies the photograph, then rings the bell. A cop comes in, Schatz murmurs a few words in his ear, the cop goes out. The Commissioner lights a Volksdeutsche and meditates.

46

"This Florian . . . Anything special about him?"

The Baron assumes a disdainful air. "Just a perfectly ordinary gamekeeper."

"Nevertheless, he had to have *something,* your gamekeeper . . . for such a great lady . . ." He picks up the photograph again and stares at it for a moment. ". . . For such a great and beautiful lady to have run off with him. . . ."

The Baron shrugs contemptuously. "I wouldn't know. If one had to pay attention to every servant . . ."

The Count doesn't share this view. "Well, as for me, Commissioner, I must confess that Florian has always seemed very strange . . . very strange indeed. First of all, he was . . . how shall I put it? Ageless. A total absence of any trace of age, and yet he often talked like someone who had seen everything and who had been around for God knows how long . . . an eternity. I have also noticed that there came from him . . . well, a certain chill. As soon as he came near, a cool shadow came upon one . . . a whiff of cold, almost glacial air. If you met him in the park—oh, he greeted you with extreme politeness; exquisite manners, that fellow had, for an ordinary gamekeeper, good, old-fashioned manners—a sort of rather sharp, penetrating little chill got hold of you, and it was rather soothing, quite pleasant, on a hot day. One felt tempted to sit down beside him, to rest and to forget, as in the cool shadow of an oak. There was something welcoming . . . inviting about him. You surely must have noticed that, my dear Baron?"

The Baron shrugs. "He was indeed an uncommonly cold person. That's all."

"Oh, come on, my friend. You once told me that you had caught pneumonia in his company."

"It was a witticism."

"All right, all right," the Commissioner cuts in. "So he gave out a little chill."

47

"A delicious one," the Count insists.

"Listen. Usually, when a woman runs away with a man, it's not because of his coldness. Anything else?"

"Yes. I told you there was something strange, something mysterious, about him. For instance, he killed flies."

"What's mysterious about that? We all kill flies, and other vermin. . . ."

The son of a bitch. I can't let that pass. I appear in front of my host and stare severely at him. Schatzchen reddens.

"I didn't mean that," he mutters. "You Jews, you only think about yourselves."

The Count is puzzled. "I beg your pardon?"

"Go on. So, this cold gamekeeper of yours, he killed flies. Anything else?"

"Oh, you see, Commissioner . . . he did not kill them in a normal, honest-to-God way."

"What do you mean, sir, killing people in a normal, honest-to-God way?"

When Schatz speaks thus with my voice, the effect is always extraordinary. As a ventriloquist, I use a kind of high falsetto, and my dummy's natural voice is a gruff baritone. You can imagine the surprise of the audience! It is an old comic effect, but it always gets a laugh.

Here I have to make a confession. I do not harass my German friend deliberately. In fact, I have sometimes the curious feeling that I myself do not exist, that it is Schatz who willingly tortures himself. Our relationship is most confusing and I must admit that I don't dare to look too deeply into it.

All I know is that my friend Schatz wishes so profoundly to get rid of me that he has even attempted suicide.

I am always afraid that he may hang himself, or turn on the gas, in a fit of anti-Semitism.

7.

DEUTSCHLAND, EIN WINTERMÄRCHEN

Schatz shuts his eyes, but he is making a big mistake: with his eyes closed, he can see me even better, because I grow then to almost legendary, mythological proportions.

He had a particularly bad time with me, last night. He screamed for help and Frau Müller immediately called the doctor. So that's what it is: the two "influential gentlemen" are psychiatrists: they are spying on him. It's all part of the plot to entrap him. For some time now he has been noticing that people look at him strangely. The reason? Perfectly obvious: after the war he let himself be de-Nazified. Today, with the German Renaissance on its way, the fact that he has been cleared by a special court of any close association with the Nazis is a black mark on his record. And what if these two have been given special orders to find out whether it is true that Commissioner Schatz is hiding a Jew?

The important thing is to keep calm, to give an impression of absolute self-control. No panic. A slightly ironic smile, just to show that you aren't duped. I know perfectly well that it is only Cohn who is trying to sow confusion and manipulate my thoughts. Even more vital, essential in fact, is it to get a firm grip on my identity: I must always remember that *I* means Schatz and no one else, whatever pressure Cohn puts

49

on me, whatever treacherous effort he makes to force me to feel that Schatz does not exist, that he is merely a figment of my tortured Jewish imagination . . . of *his* tortured German imagination. As you see, the situation is so delicate that I always keep a copy of *Who's Who* on my desk, just in case. As my old, well-beloved master, Rabbi Zur, from Bialystok—peace to his ashes—used to say, with great wisdom: "A man is a man is a man, *tfou, tfou, tfou,*" and though such a statement may sound to you a bit pessimistic and even cynical, I take this as being a frightening but indisputable truth. Who am I then, to tell you who I am? Only last week my psychiatrist tried to convince me that both Schatz and Cohn were mere phantasms, and he even implied that Cohn was a type of comical ghetto Jew who no longer existed, that both the Nazis and Israel had taken care of his kind. Who was *I* then, I wanted to know? The doctor assumed a patient expression and said that we'd have to look into that at a later stage of the treatment, but that, generally speaking, regardless of who *I* was, the *I* in question needed all the psychiatric and social care it could get. And so it is quite likely that the two men in front of me are here to examine me and report to the authorities on the state of Commissioner Schatz's mind. Doctors, quite obviously. That old witch of a Frau Müller, who hates me—everybody hates me, anti-Semites, all of them—must have reported last night's incident to my superiors. Everybody is after me, and it's quite likely that Guth is part of the plot: he wants my job. I should not have spoken to him so frankly a moment ago. Now he must be typing his report, informing on me to headquarters. *I have the honor to report that Commissioner Schatz is an impostor; that the man who has been passing as him for the last twenty years is a Jew by the name of Cohn, a situation that should be dealt with immediately. . . .*

I hear a laugh, but I am not sure whether it is he or I who

is laughing. There are moments when I no longer know who is thinking, talking, or suffering: he or I. I very much enjoy these brief moments of doubt: perhaps none of all that ever happened, and 1941 to 1944 is merely a horror story, like those of the Brothers Grimm, told to frighten our grandchildren and teach them to be good. The title of a book by the Jew Heine comes to my mind: *Deutschland, ein Wintermärchen. Germany, A Winter's Tale.* That's it: nothing but a tale, in the best tradition of *The Student of Prague,* of Dr. Mabuse, of Hoffmann, of Chamisso. A mere flight of fancy, a figment of the writer's imagination, in the impressionistic manner of Grosz, of Kurt Weill, of *Metropolis* and Conrad Veidt. And the collective responsibility of the German people is a tale too, like the collective responsibility of the Jews for the death of Jesus. There is a far greater responsibility, a far more universal guilt: I do not believe that two human beings anywhere can look each other in the face without casting down their eyes in shame. . . .

As you see, Schatz is trying to confuse you. He would like you to believe that he no longer exists, that he survives only in me and through me. He is trying to muddle up everything, to "drown the fish," as we say in Yiddish, but it is a very difficult art. It would take more than genius to suppress the millions of suppressed. All the treasures of the Louvre will never achieve that. If you take a good look at our immortal masterpieces, you will see me bursting through the pictures, my head protruding through a Rembrandt, a Vermeer, a Velázquez, a Cézanne, as though from the sewers of the Warsaw ghetto: Cuckoo! Here I am!

There are moments of supreme delusion when Schatz actually believes that he no longer has a separate physical existence, that I have assimilated him completely. He often feels that he has become completely Jewish. He even talks of his plans to settle in Israel. The other morning he did something most peculiar for a former Nazi: he pulled down his pajama trousers, took out his thing, and stared at it for a long time in astonishment: he was amazed to find that he had not yet been circumcised.

I did not go as far as that and, anyway, I couldn't: I am only able to exert a psychological influence on him, to help him morally and spiritually. I am very good at that, as you may have noticed.

I won't claim that ex-*Judenfresser* Schatz has been totally reeducated by me, but I can say without boasting that he is making good progress: I saw him the other evening prowling timidly around the Israeli Consulate in Germany, even though he wouldn't dare go in and apply for a visa. Mind you, it would be terrible to find Schatz one day in the Israeli army or police. This is his dearest hope, his golden dream: to settle in Israel and worm his way into Israel's army or secret police, and to be discovered there one day, still Schatz, but a Jewish Schatz. It would be his moment of triumph, of complete vindication.

As a matter of fact, Schatzchen's ultimate hope is to be discovered sooner or later in all and each of us, Jew, Negro, White, American, and Chinese alike. And if, in order to become a great power once more, Germany must give up anti-Semitism, she will do it. Germany is a very determined nation and not one to shrink from any sacrifice. Soon all that will be left of the past will be nostalgia: *The Diary of Anne Frank,* as you may know, was a best seller in Germany.

No, our historical relationship is not simple, our intimacy not without a cloud. The other day, Schatzchen played a dirty trick on me: he tried to kill me again. He had himself locked up for three weeks in a psychiatric clinic and had a series of electric shocks. He quite simply tried to electrocute me. I went through some terrible hours. It was one method of getting rid of me the Nazis had not attempted, and yet it was the most effective. With a good series of electric-shock treatment, there would not have been a trace of the Jews left in their minds.

At the end of two weeks, I was so weakened that I didn't even have the strength to show myself, and I think that's what saved me. Schatz could no longer see me and the doctors pronounced him cured.

He came out of the clinic with a big, happy grin. It took me about a fortnight to recover, but at last I was again able to wake him in the middle of the night and he took one look at me and went into the kitchen to make us some gefilte fish and *kneydl*. Since then he has made no further effort to get rid of me.

Now he pulls his handkerchief out of his pocket and wipes his forehead. He is determined to fight them all, tooth and nail. He is a born fighter, he proved that on the Russian front. He knows that he has been having fits of persecution mania, which is quite normal, after all: the whole world has ganged up against the Germans, trying to make them feel guilty and to undermine their moral fiber. One even begins to wonder if the massacre of the Jews was not part of a Jewish plot to give Germany a bad name and to infect us Germans with a feeling of guilt and remorse. After all, one must remember that *the Jews did not fight*. They allowed themselves to be slaughtered. Why? In order to give Germany a bad name, that's why.

"What do you mean by killing people in a normal way?"

The Count hesitates briefly. "Well, you may not believe me, but Florian didn't kill those flies, not the way you or I would. He didn't touch them. They dropped around him, just like that."

"Just like ... *what?*"

"It was very weird. As soon as a fly flew near him, it dropped dead. And the mosquitoes too. Even butterflies."

"Maybe he smelled horrible, your gamekeeper. But then, if such a great and beautiful lady went with him . . . Hm . . . Strange, indeed!"

"And the flowers. I almost forgot the flowers. The castle gardener, Johann, was on very bad terms with him. He almost accused him of killing flowers. He kept complaining to the Baron . . ."

"I really don't see the connection with the disappearance of my wife," the Baron says. "We are losing valuable time."

Schatz raises his hand. "Allow me. You said, the flowers?"

"I saw him do it. To tell the truth, I do not believe Florian meant any harm to the flowers, in fact he was very fond of them. He was always hanging around the rose bushes. It was not deliberate, but after he had been there a little while, or merely smelled the flowers, they would begin to wither away and die."

"What do you mean?"

"Like the flies."

Schatz is puzzled. "He seems to be a bit of a prankster, your gamekeeper."

"Even the birds . . . As soon as he appeared, they would start to sing—to sing very beautifully—and then they would fall silent and drop at his feet. I think it was a nervous phenomeon with him."

"And apart from this, did he have any other endearing little traits of character?"

"I didn't notice anything special. Perfectly ordinary gamekeeper. . . . Oh, yes, maybe his looks."

"Evil? Threatening?"

"Not at all. Quite on the contrary, he always looked at you . . . How shall I put it? With a certain tenderness. Yes, with sympathy and expectation. An affectionate, encouraging look, as if he expected a great deal from you."

"To drop dead, I suppose?"

"To me, personally, he was not at all unattractive. I very much liked to know that he was always there, in the park . . . waiting. His presence had something reassuring about it, peaceful, even promising. One felt that he was eager to oblige. He loved nature. The park is very beautiful and one could always find Florian waiting in the shadows. I often tried to talk to him: one felt an irresistible urge to talk philosophy to him. He answered politely, but always kept his distance. Once or twice I wanted to discuss the problem of death with him. He avoided the subject, with a kind of modesty."

"He didn't take anything with him when he left? I mean, apart from the Baroness?"

"Nothing."

"What did he look like?"

"Tall, thin, with a bony face, and, as I said before, ageless. A look of eternity. He had a rather strange way of dressing . . ."

"I spoke to him about it on several occasions," the Baron intervenes. "He dressed like one of those horrible young men who wait on the sidewalk outside of cheap hotels."

"Pimps."

"It was not at all in character. He seemed well-read, with an extraordinary grasp of history. He could recite the last words of almost all our great heroes. He was very fond of poetry and always had a book of poems in his pocket."

"You can have a taste for poetry and still be a son of a bitch. Happens all the time."

"I even think it was poetry that first brought Florian and Lily together."

"Lily. . . ?"

"That's the Baroness. She had a passion for great lyric poetry. I often saw her with Florian in the park, reading poems to each other."

The Baron looks shocked. "You ought to have told me, my dear Count. I would have put a stop to that."

"I didn't see any harm in it."

The Commissioner doesn't seem convinced. "Is that all they did together?"

The telephone rings.

"Yes? Don't shout, for Christ's sake. All right, all right. With his pants off and an expression of deep satisfaction on his face . . . Right, that makes twenty-three stiffs, all blissfully happy. *Don't sound so frustrated, Sergeant. Who knows, it could happen to you too. . . . Ha-ha-ha!*"

I know one is not supposed to laugh at one's own jokes, but I couldn't help it. As my falsetto, slightly whistling laugh issues from the mouth of Schatz, the two visitors look slightly bewildered.

Schatz laughs again, this time in his own voice, to try to cover up. I feel a bit ashamed and annoyed with myself. I mustn't give my host and buddy too much *tsuris*. But I can't help myself. I'm always trying to take him over completely. You know what they say about us Jews: give us an inch and we'll try to grab everything. As we say in Yiddish: *mea culpa*.

8.

Culture

The heat is appalling.

Schatz is covered in sweat and his shirt is soaked. His little blue eyes swivel round and round suspiciously, as he believes me to be everywhere, which I am.

"Let's hear more about this . . . Florian of yours. I'm interested."

The Count shrugs. "I saw very little of him. But whenever I had a shooting party, he was always there. Incidentally, he was the best shot I've ever seen."

"Ah, we're getting somewhere at last. And did the Baroness go . . . shooting often?"

"Never. She was only interested in one thing . . ."

"A one-track mind, huh?"

" . . . She was only interested in spiritual values."

"Was she very . . . demanding?" '

"Not at all. She had a horror of jewelry and clothes. She dressed very simply. She loved art, poetry, music, nature. Lily has very modest tastes."

"They are sometimes the most difficult to satisfy. . . . The gamekeeper now . . . was he jealous of other men? Capable of killing twenty-three men, out of jealousy?"

The Baron's face turns scarlet. He almost sobs with indignation. "I protest! I protest most emphatically! How dare you? Lily, my Lily . . . mixed up with these vulgar, abominable crimes! She was born a Schleswig-Holstein!"

"You know, the Hohenzollerns weren't bad either, and in 1914 they caused millions of deaths!"

The Baron is deeply outraged. "You have a low, monstrous, shameless mind! To imagine that a woman so well-born, such a great, truly aristocratic lady, could be in any possible way mixed up with these horrors . . . I insist that you take it all back! Lily, my Lily . . . so beautiful, so noble . . ."

"How many lovers had she before the gamekeeper?"

"None! You are drunk! She is a being of exquisite sensitivity, of a most high-minded, idealistic nature. The greatest musicians and artists were at her feet. Culture! That's what she lived for. Humanism . . . It's a thing universally known: she walked in beauty! Wagner! Beethoven! Nietzsche! Schiller! Rilke! Hölderlin! Erasmus! Those were her lovers . . . to mention only a few at random! She has inspired our greatest poets! Odes! Lyrics! Elegies! Sonnets! All have sung her beauty, her nobility, the immortal light burning in her soul. . . ."

The right word here is cremation, but I let that pass.

"Her greatness was impressed upon the young, from generation to generation, in all the schools! Our students were taught to love her, even in kindergarten! She inspired heroism and sacrifice! The only relationship she had with friends was on the highest spiritual level! She had only one purpose, one need, one aspiration: CULTURE!"

He is right, one hundred percent. CULTURE. You can't repeat that often enough.

When we were digging our grave, while the SS were leveling their machine guns, I asked my neighbor at the graveside, Sioma Kapelusznik, what he thought of culture, if he could give me a good definition of the word "culture," so that I would know I wasn't dying for nothing, but was leaving at least some kind of heritage behind me. He obliged, but all those brats yelling in their mothers' arms—the mothers who were holding their babies were excused from digging their graves—at first prevented me from hearing his answer. So, while digging, Sioma Kapelusznik moved a bit closer to me, winked and then said:

CULTURE IS WHEN MOTHERS WHO ARE HOLDING THEIR BABIES IN THEIR ARMS ARE EXCUSED FROM DIGGING THEIR OWN GRAVES BEFORE BEING SHOT.

It was a good *khokhme*, and we both had a good laugh. I'm telling you, there's no funnyman like the Jewish funnyman.

"She had only one purpose in life: culture!"

I was, I remember, a bit piqued at the thought that it was a colleague and not I who had made such a good crack before dying, so I tried to think of an even better *vitz*, but they had already started shooting us, so I had to make do with a visual effect, showing the Germans my *tokhes*. Since then, thank God, I have had all my leisure to reflect peacefully on exactly what "culture" meant, and I finally found a rather good definition, when reading the newspapers a year or so ago. At that time the German press was full of accounts of atrocities committed by the savage Simbas, in the Congo. The civilized world was indignant. So let me put it this way: the Germans had Schiller, Goethe, Hölderlin, and the Simbas of the Congo had nothing. The difference between the Germans, heirs to an immense culture, and the savage Simbas is that the Simbas ate their victims, whereas the Germans turned theirs into soap. *This need for cleanliness, that is culture.*

"All right, all right," says Schatz. "So she loved poetry. What about the rest? It seems nevertheless that she had other . . . interests."

"She had a horror of vulgarity . . . of certain . . . animal contacts."

"Husbands often believe that. What about the game-keeper?"

"He was . . . inoffensive. He had been the victim of a shooting accident in France. . . . You see what I mean?"

"What was he doing in France?"

"Well, he is a German, isn't he? He was doing his duty."

"Why should the Baroness have gone off with a eunuch?"

"Because he is harmless."

"Then one might just as well stay with one's husband."

I rub my hands. That's a good one, in the best Shwarze Shikse tradition.

Schatz freezes, his mouth wide open, terrified by what he has just said, in a thin, falsetto voice.

The two visitors are outraged.

"Sir!"

There is something so distinguished, so impeccably clean and elegant, about our aristocrats that at times I ask myself if there is a greater art than that of dressing up. Lily herself, I hasten to add, has always been admirably attired. *Kultur.* Our most inspired artists and thinkers devoted themselves to the task, so that she might dwell in beauty, like the madonna of the frescoes, the princess of the legends.

In the alcoholic haze with which Schatzchen has surrounded me, there are moments when all I am able to see of our elite is their superb attire.

"Great," the Commissioner concludes. "So they are visiting museums together, listening to Bach, reciting immortal poetry to each other. . . . Gentlemen, please let me get on with my work. A perfect couple has been found at last: an impotent lover and his frigid mistress, and you may be assured that I am not going to interfere with their happiness."

The Baron starts to roar, but his protests are drowned by

a commotion outside, a breathless, imploring voice shouting "*Herr Baron*, I've got to speak to *Herr Baron*," and the office of the Central Police Station at Number 12 Goethestrasse in Licht is brightened by a new and moving presence, and it adds to our beautiful legend that indispensable, if humble contribution: the popular touch.

9.
A Simple Soul

It's the castle gardener, Johann. I know him well: I always have three boiled eggs for breakfast, but I insist that they be very fresh, and Schatz buys them from Johann and boils them for me himself. Exactly three and a half minutes, the way I like them. I'm a bit of a stickler about that: a little more than three and a half minutes, or a little less, and Schatz gets indigestion.

Johann is a hulking young peasant who never seems to know what to do with his feet, which are enormous. He wears a straw hat and a leather apron, and he looks like someone who's just escaped from a fire.

"Herr Baron . . . Ach, Herr Baron!"

"Lily!" the Baron howls. "What's happened to Lily?"

"Herr Ba–ba–ba——"

"When you've stopped braying!" Schatz cuts in.

"Herr—ba—ba-a . . ."

"Speak up, you imbecile!"

"Lily! What has happened to Lily? Did they find her body?"

"S–s–seventeen!" roars the gardener.

"Twenty-three!" the Commissioner corrects him.

"Seventeen!" insists Johann.

"Twenty-three! We've got it all written down right here. All of them beaming and all of them with their pants off."

"Seventeen," the gardener repeats stubbornly. "I counted them myself. They were all over the place. In Florian's cottage . . . in the greenhouse . . . all over the park!"

There is a moment of horrified silence.

"Good God!" bellows Schatz. "They aren't the same corpses! That makes forty!"

"When Florian disappeared . . . we went into his cottage. . . . We found . . . bodies! B–bones! All over the place! In the oven! In the furnace! The jockey . . . *Herr Baron,* you remember Sanders, the jockey who disappeared? He was there! All dressed for a race—just like when he rode *Herr Baron's* mare! He was still wearing *Herr Baron's* racing colors! And there was a postman, with his bag still full of warm mail, a bicycle racer . . ."

"A bicycle racer?" the Commissioner shouts. "That's Sprintz! You remember, he started the great Tour of Germany race and never showed up anywhere!"

"Three firemen . . . four Negro GI's . . . two truck drivers . . . six clean towels . . . one watering can . . . six demitasse spoons . . . a salt shaker and a fork . . ."

"Wait a minute, wait a minute!" roars Schatz. "He's lost his head. What do you expect her to do with a salt shaker and a fork?"

"Sir!" roars the Baron. "You can't be talking about Lily, I hope?"

"My poor, dear, noble friend, you must be brave," implores the Count.

"One road sweeper . . . one plumber . . . seven clean shirts . . . She who was always so pure and so gentle!"

"Who, *she?*" bellows the Baron.

I shrug. I really don't see what the fuss is about. It's nothing new and not even peculiar to Germany: a devouring yearning, a heroic ambition, and a misplaced belief in their system, in their know-how, in their virility. Millions of heroes fucked themselves dead trying to fuck humanity happy. It's been going on since the beginning of yearning. Look at the French . . . and they're supposed to be great lovers.

The Baron sits there, blinking, unable to bring himself to face the truth about his Lily, at last; the Count keeps mopping his pale forehead with a shaking hand, while the good Johann continues his epic tale:

"And in the greenhouse, *Herr Baron* . . . Florian hasn't even bothered to hide the bodies. They still smelled nice . . . Her Ladyship's own perfume. Four happy stiffs lying on the floor . . . She had just finished with them . . . they were lying there, still beaming. Such grins, *Herr Baron!* Such dirty grins! Their eyes were wide open . . . as if they were still looking at it. . . . She had shown it to them, her little absolute. Those good Germans were allowed to see her little absolute, to touch it, to fondle it, to hold it, they died knowing that it truly existed, that it wasn't merely the opium of the people. . . ."

And now he starts to cry, the gardener Johann. "I swear to you, *Herr Baron*, those lucky stiffs, they knew what they died for!"

Hübsch has risen, he leans forward, his face twisted by nervous spasms.

"All with their asses bare?" the Commissioner asks curtly.

"All of them! Such happy little birdies!"

"Birdies?" repeats Schatz. "What birdies? Where?"

"Little birdies huddled in their nests and happy-shmappy, after their last song!"

"Happy-shmappy, eh?" asks Schatz, his voice thick, his eyes bloodshot. "This merciless Jew is sapping the German moral fiber again."

"What Jew?" the Baron asks.

This time Schatz lets himself go. I try to hold him back— if he gives away our little secret, they will lock him up again, and what with their new drugs that may well be the end of me. But Schatz is in such a state of mental stress that he throws all prudence overboard.

"Gentlemen, I must warn you: we have fallen into the hands of a third-rate Yiddish music-hall clown, by the name of Genghis Cohn, who is dancing his revengeful Jewish *hora* on our German honor!"

He is asking for it. I rush out and perform a very quick little dance in front of Schatzchen. Tap-tap-tap! go my heels on the floor, tap-tap-tap! The two aristocrats, their mouths wide open, stare at the chief of the Licht police. It is not often that one sees a German Commissioner of the *erste Klasse,* even in an advanced state of alcoholic delirium, dance the *hora* in front of two distinguished visitors.

As for me, I am delighted. It took me more than twenty years' effort to make Schatzchen perform this little Jewish dance. But it was well worth it. I relax and watch him go tap-tap-tap! on the floor of the police station. Then my old craving for artistic perfection gets hold of me again: should I or should I not make him sing *Yiddishe Mamme* for the two psychiatrists who have been asked to examine Commissioner *erste Klasse* Schatz discreetly, to check on the rumor that his guilt feelings have driven him *erste Klasse* mad?

Or should I perhaps run to a synagogue and beg ten pious Jews to pray for me and liberate my Jewish soul from its German dybbuk? I mean: to liberate my German soul from the clutches of a Jewish dybbuk?

The most important thing right now is to recover my sense of identity. There are moments when I begin to feel that both of us are merely *humans, tfou, tfou, tfou,* and thus the Nazi is capable of turning up in the Jew and the Jew in the Nazi: we are both part of the very semen of the species.

The Commissioner *erste Klasse* has collapsed into his chair. Alcohol gives a crooked, twisted, unreal character to all things

65

around him, and the world appears so abominable that it begins to look like reality. He knows that the only way to prove his sanity is to carry on with the official business at hand. The murders in the Forest of Geist are filling every decent man with indignation. Forty deaths can be counted, it is something you can grasp, even visualize. If there were sixty million victims, people would have been less shocked. Such a figure would be a mere abstraction.

He checks the total again. "Twenty-three in the forest, plus seventeen in the park, that makes forty . . ."

Johann the gardener is a stickler for details. "Plus the salt-shaker, plus . . ."

This time, the Baron admits the evidence. "My God!" he bellows. "My wife has been unfaithful to me!"

Johann the gardener twists his straw hat in his hands. His face is all wet with tears. He is a simple soul and he knows, with the unfailing instinct of simple people, what there is on this earth that can truly measure up to the old human craving for perfection. He raises a finger, points it into space, here it is, the little German absolute: Johann the gardener is one of our true visionaries.

"It's all golden and warm and open and beckoning, it's there, it exists, it's not merely the opium of the people!"

The clerk is petrified. His rigidity reminds one of prehistoric statues, of great pagan cults. He, too, seems to see Her Ladyship's little absolute, gleaming and beckoning somewhere out there, among our other guiding lights. The spectacles on his nose sparkle, his collar stud has shot off, he gulps. His romantic and spiritual needs are of such urgency and magnitude that all he needs now to answer the call of Germania is a nuclear warhead. Suddenly I notice in him an astonishing phallic resemblance to Himmler: it's exactly the same face. In a flash I see a hundred thousand new and rigid NPD party members standing to attention under the banners of Nuremberg, bulging with virility after twenty-five years of democratic flabbiness, ready to try again, desperately eager to give their beloved that total fulfillment she has been so desperately longing for, the final solution of all her woes.

10.

The Return
to
the Sources

The heat is such that little icy shivers are running up and down my spine. There's a smell of ram, of superman, in the air: a new historical rut is in preparation. Already Deputy Fasbender of the *Nazional Partei Deutschland's* is screaming to the press, like in the good old times: "You'll soon stop making fun of us!" Already the Socialist Willy Brandt, accused of having been a dogged anti-Nazi in the Hitler days, has felt obliged to join the Kiesinger Government, to rid himself of that nasty reputation. "Germany Must Become Herself Again," proclaim the NPD posters, and an enthusiastic crowd applauds wildly along the Stations of the Cross at Oberammergau, a classic show in which hatred and respect for historical truth have accomplished a real miracle, a real Resurrection: not yet that of Christ, of course, but at least that of the lowly Jew reborn from his German ashes and pushing our Lord and Saviour Jesus Christ toward the gas chamber. I'm deeply moved. I appreciate that respect for traditional values, for our cultural blue chips. They're reinvesting. Twenty-four years after *Jew Süss* the good citizens of Oberammergau roll up their sleeves, get on with the job, and resuscitate the Jew they are accused of having exterminated. They have given me back my historical place, assigned me back to my ignoble image: nothing is missing on the face of the actor who plays Judas, no spittle, no baseness, no ignominy. One senses the hand of an expert, an authentic and classical inspiration, two thousand years of practice. They had some trouble finding a realistic enough actor among the good citizens of Oberammergau, an actor with a real Jewish nose, real Jewish ears, the shifty eyes and the typical libidinous lips I have always been given by the great old masters of religious art.

I'm afraid they'll go even further. I fear the worst: I fear they'll offer me their brotherhood. They're capable of anything, even of claiming me as one of their own. Come with us, Jew: be a member. Until now they massacred us, but at least that spared us their company, that was how, in medieval times, we managed to escape chivalry. Declaring us unworthy to bear a sword, they left commerce and usury to us: thus we were able to avoid dishonor. One will look in vain for us among the noble knights, the Saint-Louis's, the Simon de Montforts, the Napoleons, the Hitlers, the Stalins, and other history makers. We were excluded from the nobility. The golden legends, the admirable historical tapestries, those were not for us. But suddenly there looms over our heads a new and horrifying menace, one which opens the ranks of chivalry and arches of triumph to us as well. Is our experience still searing enough in our memory and in our blood to help us resist the temptation? Or shall we Jews become crusading knights, heroes, and conquerors too? I don't want to think about it. I don't have to, as a matter of fact. The future, thank God, no longer exists for me. I belong to the past. I'm a little comical Jew of the old Yiddish burlesque, a *khokhem* who was censored once and for all in 1943, and if you are old enough, and were interested enough in ghetto folklore, you

69

may have seen me at the Shwarze Shikse, the Mottke Ganeff, or at the Mitornisht Sorgen. I may even have had the honor and pleasure of making you laugh at the time, and perhaps you now feel ashamed of having laughed at me. Have no regrets. As Montaigne said, laughter is a deeply human characteristic.

11.

She Is Beyond My Means

You see that I have my worries, my *tsuris*, in spite of my breeziness. Fortunately, I am rescued from my meditations by Johann the gardener. This simple soul has that rare gift of being able to reduce the absolute to more human proportions, I would even say that he reduces it to its barest and must humble expression. Clasping his straw hat to his heart, he points his finger at something which only he can see, with all the fervor and naiveté of the true believer.

"Oh, it's so pretty, it's so soft. . . . Oh, Her Ladyship! The lovely, fluffy, sweet little nest! Look, it's so fair, all golden!"

"We are being covered with filth!" exclaims the Baron. "Trampled underfoot! I can smell the poisonous miasma of unmentionable pornography, of some dreadful Jewish obscenity!"

I sniff: there is, in fact, a slight odor of gas. Nothing very important: small caresses, breezes, a humble cultural trace of the passage of our princess of the legends, of our madonna of the frescoes.

"How generous! How sweet! How lavishly she gives, how charitable she is! How she loves to make people happy! They all looked so contented, *Herr Baron!* Only . . . Why everybody else and not me? Why a watering can, a salt shaker, and six pairs of socks, a bicycle pump and the little mailman with his mail still warm, and not me?"

"It's rattled him," the Commissioner remarks. "He's had a traumatic shock."

"Lily! My Lily was leading a double life!" sobs the Baron.

"Double?" queries the Commissioner.

"Pull yourself together, dear, noble friend," the Count implores him. "Keep your faith in her. I'm convinced she did it from the highest motives! Who knows, perhaps reasons of state were involved? Don't forget that during the war we too had to commit certain reprehensible acts. We were motivated by ideological reasons!"

The clerk is only biting his fists, but one feels he already has more ambitious plans. Under the bureaucrat's skin lurks a fanatic. Only a Fuehrer could guide such male ardor to its natural goal. There has to be an end to the flabbiness of democracies, the NPD should be given power, should thrust forward its million members, guide their virility to a triumphant fulfillment, the end of longing. A vague erection in the state of Hesse or in Bavaria isn't enough. Hübsch is fascinated, standing to attention so rigidly that the air itself becomes permeated with the headiness of final solutions: this is the end of brief encounters, one-night stands, of cooing, wooing, and yearning. *Kennst du das Land wo die Zitronen blühn, in dunkeln Laub die Gold-Orangen glühn.* . . . At Marzobotto, in Italy, two thousand women and children were exterminated by the supermen in a last spasm of virility. And Johann the gardener keeps adding fuel to the flame.

"Oh, the pretty little fluffiness, the darling little nest, all pink and so cuddly! How sweet and how welcoming . . . I'm willing. Oh, yes, I'm willing."

This confession is moving because it comes from the little people. Not the workers and not the middle class, but just between the two, and it's comforting to know that they are willing. The legendary princess can feel reassured. She

72

will never be in want. They'll march forward in close ranks, their morale high and their hearts on their sleeves, and they'll let themselves be slaughtered, trying to satisfy her.

The clerk's tongue is hanging out, his hormones are aboil. The Commissioner bangs with his fist.

"Hübsch! That's enough! Down! Down! They're trying to destroy us. It's the Chinese. I tell you, it's the Chinese. They have a secret weapon. Poison gas. It creates a state of paralysis, you stiffen, you can't move! Meanwhile, they launch their paratroops! There's something going on here that isn't very kosher!"

I swear I didn't make him say that.

The Count adjusts his monocle. "Florian must have some powerful reasons."

"Now, that's enough," shrieks the Commissioner. "Enough pornography!"

"If he kills," the Count continues, "if he really is the author of this massacre, then it must be for a worthy cause. I would even say, a noble cause. The fellow's always seemed a bit of an idealist to me. I'm sure he's incapable of killing for other than an inspired reason."

I make an appearance on the scene. As soon as someone invokes *reasons* for a massacre, I come trotting on and introduce myself. I don't mind having been killed for no reason whatsoever, with no excuse whatsoever, somehow I feel less indignant. But as soon as someone mentions a doctrine, an ideology, a cause, I make my appearance, with my yellow star, my face still covered with plaster. My friend Schatz looks at me with something bordering on despair. He's wrong. One should never despair. Just give it to her more radically. One race isn't enough, or one class, or one country. You have to give her all you have. Lily can take a lot. And there are bound to be some survivors.

73

"Cohn, get the hell out of here," Schatz cries. "I'm sick of your *shtik*. I call that real exhibitionism. You begin to be a pain in the neck with your guilty conscience. All right, you forced us to do some ghastly things to you. We forgive you. It's only in bad detective novels that the guilty return to the scene of their crime. You've already done Germany enough harm for the last quarter of a century with your propaganda. Now I'm willing to forget it all, but only on condition that you get off our backs! I'll tell you something, Cohn. You're out of date. You're old-fashioned. We've seen enough of you. Lily wants something new. Your yellow stars, your ovens, your gas chambers, nobody wants to hear about them anymore. Lily wants something different, something really thrilling. We want to keep moving forward. Auschwitz, Treblinka, Belsen, it's beginning to be a cliché. That's 'Daddy's Jews.' The young don't give a damn about all that anymore. The young, they were born with the atomic bomb, with the promise of a thousand suns in their eyes. For them, your concentration camps seem a farce. They've had enough of your Jewish odds and ends, your messy little tidbits. So stop trying to hang onto your little capital of suffering, to your miserable investments and savings, try to make yourself more interesting. Lily can get a hundred million at one go, my friend, so whom are you trying to impress with your old six million?"

Touché. This time he hit the bull's-eye. I am forced to admit that I lack capital. Lily is beyond my means. She's a great lady, a princess, she has the right to be demanding. I'm the victim of inflation. I feel suddenly ruined, diminished. Everything I've accumulated and preserved so painfully throughout the centuries isn't enough. Today, she can have a hundred, a hundred and fifty million, just by pushing on a button. Thousands of buildings, entire cities. I'm completely devalued, I'm bankrupt, I don't count anymore. I pull painfully together what's left of my dignity and my importance and go off in a corner to sulk. She doesn't want us Jews, very well. She wants the Chinese, very well. I know what it is. Discrimination. Anti-Semitism, that's what it is.

12.

A Bloody
Nymphomaniac

Schatz is feeling a little better. He's lost sight of me. He rubs his hands together and hums a little tune. He's recovered from the fit of "obsessional hallucination," as his doctor calls it, and is once again in contact with reality. He looks it straight in the face, eyes wide open, no paranoiac generalizations, and sees things as they are in all their simplicity, that is to say: a cuckolded idealist, a frigid nymphomaniac who longs for fulfillment, a salt shaker, a watering can, six little spoons, an assassin who kills all who fail to give Lily satisfaction, a little postman still full of warm mail, a family friend, and an unhappy gardener, slightly feeble-minded, who sees our legendary princess bare-assed, which vision plunges him into a state of erotic delirium. All of this embellished by Michelangelo, who thrusts a horrified head out of a sewer in the Warsaw ghetto. No wonder that Schatz is suspicious of reality, that he has the impression someone is playing a gross practical joke upon him. One thing, anyway, is certain: the legendary princess serves as bait, the spout of the watering can is twisted, the salt shaker is only there to allay suspicion, and all these bits and pieces of evidence put together bear witness to some subversive and hateful art, which seeks to mock and to defile, a true return of the flames of decadent Jewish expressionism.

As for me, I couldn't care less. They're getting along very well without me. I am rather moved by Johann, though: I like visionaries. We're all of us sensitive to beauty and easily troubled by it: but it's not so much the thing he sees that astonishes me, it's the dimensions.

"Hey, gardener! gardener!" shouts the Commissioner. "There's nothing at all over there on the horizon, or in any case, not *that*. It's all in your head! You're a sex maniac!"

"But, the watering can, *Herr Baron*, sir? You should have seen in what shape she left it. All twisted!"

"I beg your pardon?" says the Count, impressed all the same.

"And six pairs of clean socks with nobody in them! Disappeared! Vanished, evaporated into happiness, all of them! All except me! Why didn't she let me try, *Herr Baron?* Why a watering can and not me? Why despise a son of the people? The bicycle pump twisted, the rubber watering hose melted, twelve volumes of the *Encyclopædia Britannica,* and not me. . . . It's undemocratic, *Herr Baron!* She doesn't have the right to treat an honest worker that way!"

Schatz goes into action. He knows, at last, who the criminals are, and he's not going to let them get away with it. He has a once-in-a-lifetime case, and he's determined to show what he can do. He grabs Lily's photograph, calls Guth, and gives orders.

"Circulate a description of this woman everywhere. And warn every man capable of . . . of bearing arms, not to approach her alone, for any reason, without a pass from the military authorities or an order of requisition——"

"What do you mean, requisition?" inquires the Count, astonished. "Requisition of *what?*"

"No one is to touch her without a draft call or an appeal for volunteers. It is forbidden to approach her, is that understood? She is vicious."

"Vicious?" bawls the Baron. "Lily is vicious? Sir, I demand satisfaction."

"So does she, apparently. Guth, be very careful. We're dealing with a dangerous, frigid nymphomaniac, who looks for a superman and happiness, and that can only lead to mass murders."

"Sir, how dare you speak of a great lady in such a manner? Shakespeare, Homer, Beethoven——"

"I know, I know. Very ancient nobility. Cathedrals everywhere. Symphonies. Libraries. It seems that's not enough for her."

"Why, she was born——"

"A Schleswig-Holstein."

"Her family is known and respected everywhere. It counts among its members——"

I giggle.

The Commissioner pounds on the desk with his fist. "Cohn, for God's sake," he says simply.

". . . Gutenberg, Erasmus, Luther, twenty-two popes, illustrious scientists, one salt shaker, one bicycle pump . . . Saints and benefactors by the thousands!"

"Yes, well . . . they couldn't manage it, the saints and the benefactors. She's still yearning."

"She's a cousin of Albert Schweitzer! He adored her! Nobel Prize winners, writers of genius . . . Lily! My Lily, a nymphomaniac . . . I can't believe it! Lily would never deceive me. Besides, perhaps nothing at all has happened. There isn't any proof. . . ."

I take a newspaper that is lying on a chair, and I put it on the desk. On the first page, there are Vietnamese corpses, maimed children, a burning village. In fact, I didn't really take up the newspaper: it was already on the desk. I simply walked up to the Commissioner, discreetly, and I pointed to the pictures with my finger. Only to help him: since the high-minded elite tends to disregard reality, there are proofs. But my action only seems to exasperate Schatz, I don't know why.

"Oh, no! Vietnam, thank God, that's not here! That's in America! What are you trying to do, Cohn? What right have you to interfere? There aren't any Jews in Vietnam. It's none of your business."

The Baron is outraged. "Commissioner, just exactly what does Vietnam have to do with all this? Surely you aren't going to mix Lily up in that too, are you? She's never set foot there! Why not accuse her of crucifying Christ while you're at it?"

Commissioner Schatz doesn't pay him the least attention. He can't stand it anymore. All those books, all those documents, all those survivors, reminiscences, and, into the bargain, his own personal Jew who's never off his back, despite psychiatric care and alcohol. Maybe he shouldn't have shouted "Fire!" twenty-four years ago. But he was young, he had an ideal, he believed in what he was doing. Today he wouldn't do it. If they were to give him a second chance, when the NPD comes into power, and if Herr von Thadden ever gave Schatz the order to shout "Fire!" well, he, Schatz . . . as a matter of fact, what would he do? He gives me a searching look, but I know better than to advise him: afterwards, they'll begin to say that we Jews sapped the moral fiber of the German people.

Schatz raises his head, looks around him with the expression of a wounded bull. He doesn't even try to hide me anymore. What good would that do? He knows that he's going to lose his job, and maybe they'll lock him up in a clinic. Commissioner Schatz has lost his mind, they'll say pityingly, as the result of Jewish persecution. But Schatz knows he isn't crazy. He knows the truth about his case, and he knows that this truth is terrible.

13.

The Dybbuk

There are but a very few things I haven't already taught my friend Schatz about our history and our beliefs, and he knows all there is to know about that familiar phenomenon, which everyone who has studied our tradition has come across: the dybbuk. Schatz, Commissioner First Class, knows that he is possessed by a dybbuk. It is an evil spirit, a demon who grabs you, gets within you, and starts to reign and lord it over you, as master. To drive him away, one needs prayers, ten pious Jews, venerable ones, known for their saintliness, who will throw their weight into the balance and chase the demon away.

Schatz has often spent hours prowling around a synagogue, but he's never dared to go inside. The truth is that this is the first time in the history of thought and religion that a pure Aryan, a former SS, has been possessed by a Jewish dybbuk. I suppose I'll have to go find myself a rabbi and plead to be delivered from my horrible destiny: being obliged to haunt the German conscience. That's the reason why normally Schatz waits on me, hand and foot. He wants to coax me. He wants me to free him, under pretext of freeing myself. But this time, with the help of alcohol and exasperation, he has really thrown caution to the winds. He can't control himself anymore. He's not even afraid of being seen by witnesses talking to a murdered Jew who isn't there.

"Listen, Cohn, you're taking advantage of this situation. First of all, I have been de-Nazified. I have papers to prove it. And besides, I want you to know that I drink to forget, not to remember. People drink, Cohn, to *forget*. Now beat it, and fast. The whole thing's beginning to smell like blackmail. It's provocation. One of these days I'm going to get angry and I'm going to show you that, despite your very special condition, you aren't untouchable. I'll give you such a beating . . . If only to prove that I have no remorse. Hard like a rock."

At these words the Count, glancing with compassion at the unfortunate Baron, murmurs tactfully:

"Watch your language!"

"I resent that," roars the Baron. "I won't let myself be insulted! Those are perfectly outrageous insinuations!"

"So get out of here, Cohn," says the Commissioner, talking to himself, pointing toward the door. "You think that because we scrawled a few swastikas here and there, because we desecrated a few graves, we need you here in Germany, that you can make yourself useful again . . . Out! Beat it!"

"He has hallucinations," remarks the Count.

"Here, kitty, kitty," says Johann, curling his finger at the teasing little absolute that he seems to see so clearly, with all the willingness of the little people who only need a leader to give her happiness at last.

Schatz buries his head in his hands. "It's not even possible to have a quiet drink anymore," he mutters.

"You really ought to stop that," says the Count. "You have delirium tremens."

"The lucky bastards who get delirium tremens see spiders and snakes and rats, but me . . ." He gives me a somber glance, full of swastikas. "Me . . . I see dead Jews."

He pushes me back, sighs deeply, then rings his buzzer.

A cop enters, goose-stepping, and salutes.

"Chief?"

"Nothing. I just wanted to see something healthy, something simple, clean . . ."

"Thanks, Chief."

The cop salutes again, does an about-face and leaves. The two doctors—Schatz is certain now that's what they are—are aghast. They've never seen a case like this before. In their entire careers they have never seen a German, a former SS, haunted by a Jewish dybbuk. They aren't even sure that it is a dybbuk. For them, no doubt, the Commissioner is having a bout of paranoiac hallucinations, based on solid, historical experiences. But the patient presents a particularly delicate problem of ethics. Schatz knows that the two psychiatrists, aware of the precedent created by Dr. Mengle and his genocide colleagues, are asking themselves whether they have the right to cure a German citizen of his remorse, if the eventual suppression of his guilt complex wouldn't be interpreted as a rebirth of Nazism. Do German doctors have the right to liquidate a Jewish *dybbuk?* It is certain that from a strictly nationalistic viewpoint, the final solution to a problem raised by six million psychic parasites of the German conscience is a desirable thing, a requirement of public hygiene. New drugs, particularly prazimine, for example, in large doses, have proven deeply efficient in this particular domain. But this new suppression of suppressed Jews can only be a governmental decision. The new German government must face its responsibilities. It must free the German conscience from its Jewish parasites. Anyway, everyone knows that the Jews weren't assassinated. They died *voluntarily*. I keep abreast of the news, as I have nothing else to do, and I recently discovered some reassuring evidence about that in the book of a certain Jean-François Steiner, *Treblinka:* We stood obligingly in line, in front of the gas chambers, we never resisted extermination. There were but a few rebels, here and there, particularly in the Warsaw ghetto, but as a whole, there was an eager, obedient will to disappear. There was a will to die. Collective suicide, that's what it was. Soon a new best-seller will demonstrate that the Nazis were only an instrument in the hands of smart Jewry. You see, Jews who wanted to die, while making some profit on the side. How? I'll tell you how. We didn't commit suicide with our own hands, as the insurance company wouldn't pay up, and our survivors couldn't have recovered any damages. So . . . It is time someone wrote a definitive work on this question, showing how we manipulated the Germans, both to make a profit and to satisfy our perverted taste for self-destruction. Somewhere there must be an author willing to unveil our diabolical maneuver, and describe how we transformed the Nazis into a blind and obedient tool in our hands.

"Feet," says the Commissioner.

"I beg your pardon?"

"I feel enormous feet on my face, hairy and circumcised. . . ."

"He's having hallucinations. It's the final stage."

"I can feel them on my face. . . . Feet, I tell you, feet without heart or pity. . . . What do they want from me? I'm an obedient, zealous official. I shouted 'Fire!' because I had orders! I had orders! Orders, Cohn. I only did my duty. I wish to be cleared of these accusations once and for all. All I want is to feel clean."

Clean? *Jawohl*, very good, at your service. I instantly appear in front of Schatz, soap in hand. I like to help people. I'm a good dybbuk. The Commissioner notices the bar of soap, screams, jumps up, knocking over his chair.

"Soap? Why soap? For twenty years I haven't touched a bar of soap. No! *You never know who's in it!*"

I hold the soap under his nose, with an inviting gesture. The Commissioner points at it with a trembling hand.

"Who is that, huh?" he screams. "Who is it, that soap?"

I shrug my shoulders. How should I know? It was mass production, they made soap wholesale, nobody marked *Jasza Geshundheit* or *Tsatsa Sardinenfish* on it. Those were difficult times. Germany was short of essential commodities.

"I refuse," bellows the Commissioner. "It looks filthy, your soap. It's not a good, honest, Catholic soap. . . ."

Oh, for Pete's sake! If he needs Catholic soap now, they are six hundred million, the Catholics. . . . Such a figure is beyond my means. Why doesn't he apply to the Chinese? But he's mistaken. This is luxury soap. I heard an SS at Auschwitz admit it himself, with a big belly laugh. *"This is a de luxe cake of soap, because it was made with the chosen people."* In German, a *khokhme* is called a *Witz*. I put my soap back in my pocket and sink deeper into Schatzchen's subconscious.

14.

The Dance
of
Genghis Cohn

"What soap? What are you talking about?"

The Commissioner remembers that he is surrounded by spies. They are all over his skin. He takes a handkerchief from his pocket and wipes his forehead. Above all, he must give the impression of assurance, of fortitude. Besides, his fears are groundless. No one suspects him, no one knows about his associate: he has always managed to hide him deep in the darkest corner of his apartment and he never left the place without making sure that his partner was securely locked in. The two personalities helping him with his inquiry on the crimes in the Forest of Geist are well known, and they play an honorable part in German cultural and social affairs, they can't be spies, *agents provocateurs*. Schatz feels completely reassured. He'll show them he can handle the situation. Coolheaded. In full control. Alert.

"Of course, you aristocrats never even got your hands dirty. You kept yourselves carefully apart in your castles, waiting for it all to pass. The elite. You didn't raise a little finger, one way or the other. But I'm a man of the people. We're the ones who are always trying to please her, to fulfill her yearnings, and we're the ones she always blames afterwards."

"What do you mean, she? Lily had nothing to do with it! I repeat that you have absolutely no proof," roars the Baron.

"Forty victims . . ."

The telephone rings. The Commissioner listens and hangs up.

"Forty-one. The captain of the football team, our best end!"

The Baron bristles with indignation. "My dear Commissioner, I must protest against these odious insinuations with the utmost vehemence," he hollers. "You speak to me of this hideous slaughter, but I speak to you of my honor! One can very well kill a few people without being an unfaithful wife! You have no right whatsoever to imagine the worst! One can have an ideology, political opinions, and still remain an honest woman!"

"What do you mean, political opinions?"

"Since these are mass murders without any apparent motivation, then there must be a doctrine behind them, an ideology, perhaps even reasons of state. Florian undoubtedly wanted a certain cause to triumph, defended certain ideas. You don't kill systematically if you don't have a system. He must be at the head of one of those political groups like the *heilig Wähme* after the First World War, which desires a strong nation, free of its internal enemies and master of its destiny. One does not kill systematically without a system. This tragedy smells of a great cause. Florian is probably the head of a political organization with ambitious aims, and no doubt he believes in what he is doing. Of course, Lily was wrong to follow a fanatic. But she has always been a romantic at heart."

Schatz no longer listens. He finds himself trapped in a real chamber of horrors. A decadent, typically Jewish expression-ism is getting hold of reality, as if some ghastly Chagall has taken possession of it. A Hasid of the Vitebsk ghetto sits on top of the filing cabinet; he has the face of Genghis Cohn and plays the violin, while a cow flies above the official por-trait of President Luebke. Hideous Soutines twist on the walls, nudes by Modigliani insult the eyes of our pure, gold-plaited *Mädchen*. Freud worms his way into the cellar and is going to reduce to filth all our art treasures. Repulsive Negro masks form a James Ensor procession, followed by a salt-shaker and a bicycle pump, and instantly compose a cubist picture. *They* are coming back. *Deutschland erwache!* March forward, Herr von Thadden, and your *Nazional Partei Deut-schland's*.

But there is worse, much worse. I am aware that Schatz no longer feels sure of his own appearance. It is as if some re-vengeful hand has risen from the mass graves and is turning him into a caricature of a German, in the manner of Georg Grosz and comparable only in its obscenity to the caricature of the beastly Jew which the world has been forcing like a mask upon the faces of the children of Israel for the last two thousand years.

"Gevalt! Rakhmones!"

Mazel tov. Allow me to congratulate myself. A good ven-triloquist is not such a common thing as it may seem, and it takes talent finally to make a German speak the words of Jewish suffering.

I try to keep my mouth shut but when Schatz gets nasty there's no stopping him.

Hate, that's what it is. Pure, merciless hate. Racists, all of them. There is obviously a Jewish conspiracy afoot: they are trying to turn us Germans into the world's new Jews. Two thousand years of persecution are about to begin.

"Gevalt! He's making me speak Yiddish again!"

I make him a little concession. I give Schatzchen back twenty percent of his thoughts and all of his own voice . . . well, maybe not quite all of it. I keep twenty-five percent for myself. One has to make a living somehow.

Schatz breathes a little more easily. For the last few minutes he has been speaking Yiddish to the two psychiatrists with such fluency that cold shivers were beginning to run down his spine: what will Herr von Thadden and the NPD leadership think of him? After all, the new Fuehrer has just declared to the press that there is no longer a Jewish problem left in Germany.

"Ho-ho-ho!" I have to laugh. No longer a Jewish problem left in Germany? How do you like that?

"Commissioner, why are you laughing?"

"Do you hear voices, Commissioner?"

"Voices, shmoices," Schatz grumbles scornfully.

"Puss, puss, puss!" the gardener Johann calls tenderly, and no man has ever had such a down-to-earth, realistic vision of paradise.

"This devil, Genghis Cohn," mutters Schatz, "was performing in a filthy literary cabaret in Warsaw and he was well known for his blue jokes . . ."

The telephone rings and Schatz grabs it, without suspecting for one instant that I may be at the other end.

"Hello? Yes . . . Are you sure? Don't forget that she belongs to our oldest and proudest family. . . . Erasmus, Schiller . . . Albert Schweitzer was a cousin. . . . No possible mistake? Right. Release her picture to the press. This time Germany must be put on its guard, so that it doesn't start all over again. . . . Thanks."

The Commissioner hangs up. His expression has become a little sad. He looks at the husband with a certain sympathy.

"Your wife's fingerprints have been found."

"Where?" stammers the Baron. *"On what* were they found?"

"Let's say: on the bodies. There's no doubt that she lent a hand. That explains the expression of bliss on the faces of these unhappy bastards."

The good Johann is enraged. "What unhappy bastards? It is the most beautiful, the most enviable fate . . . I . . . I want her fingerprints! I want them all over me!"

The clerk has collapsed into his chair. He is in an alarming state of availability. I go up to him and stroke his hair. Good boy. Don't worry, you will get your Fuehrer.

The Baron is still fighting the evidence, with the blue-eyed determination of an authentic idealist.

"It doesn't prove a thing," he shouts. "She may have left her fingerprints whilst defending herself against rape. Germany too has been raped by the Nazis. Humanity has often had to submit to a fate worse than death, after a last desperate stand! Those brutes probably attacked her. There was a hand-to-hand fight, which explains the fingerprints. The gamekeeper arrived and killed them. He was doing his duty."

"Forty-one dead, you must be joking!"

The Baron has a last moment of beautiful hope. "And then, these beastly men may have been killed . . . before. Nothing proves that the act was consummated. There is no proof that I have been dishonored."

"They were killed in a state of absolute bliss."

"It's a calumny, Commissioner, they are trying to cover us with mud. This whole business stinks of malice, venom, and premeditation. Since our enemies are gone . . . they do nothing but libel us. They even created a state with that sole purpose. Have you read all those horrors that man Wiesenthal printed in his books?"

This time Schatz agrees wholeheartedly. "True, they trample on our faces, they dance their Asiatic scalp dance on our good German name, a dance of vengeance and hate, under the orders of the chief of this ghastly, merciless Gestapo, Genghis Cohn!"

Whizz—bang—tra-la-la! I fling myself forward, my arms folded, and I dance my Asiatic scalp dance, our old *hora* here, in the heart of Germany, in the city of Licht, near the Forest of Geist, 12 Goethestrasse, not to mention Lessing, Schiller, Nietzsche, Bach, and all the other face-saving names they thrust forward to save Lily's reputation after each *Walpurgiensnacht*. I have always been rather good at dancing, but I dance even better now that I have practically no weight other than that of memory. I leap in the air, I click my heels, I slap my boots with my hands, one-two-three, hop! one-two-three, hop! It is a mixture of Russian *kazachok,* which we had learned from watching the Cossacks of the Ukraine dancing in our villages after a pogrom, and our old Jewish *hora.* What a pity Schatzchen is the only one who can see me. He shrinks back, horrified, then points at me.

"Do you see him? This has been going on for the last twenty-four years. I cannot get rid of him. I've tried everything."

"Who are you talking about?"

The Commissioner shuts up at once. It's his misfortune to have become acquainted with me, after the execution: he should never have looked into the file, bothered to find out who the defiant Jew was who showed him his bare ass when the order "Fire!" rang out, instead of getting killed nicely and quietly. When you kill, let us say a thousand people, it's anonymous, a mere figure, an abstraction. You can burn a million people without remorse: the figure is so huge it becomes meaningless. There is no difference between sixty million dead and six million: your feelings do not increase or decrease proportionately. But it's a different matter when you become personally familiar with one of them. It's catching.

In a way I should be thankful to Schatzchen: he rescued me from oblivion by catching me. I don't say, mind you, that the subconscious of a former Nazi is a place in the sun, but it is better than nothing.

Now, Johann the gardener taps his forehead.

"Oh yes, there were more of them in the park, under the rose bushes. Young men, students, here and there, lying around, in romantic poses . . . There was one who was holding a bicycle pump . . ."

"A bicycle pump," the Commissioner notes dutifully. "She doesn't stop at anything."

"What on earth do you want her to do with a bicycle pump?" the Baron groans.

"I don't know. It takes all kinds. She was probably getting desperate."

"I object!" the Baron explodes. "Let me remind you that you are speaking of a being whose incomparable greatness has surpassed all our thoughts and some of our best writing. I have poems which prove it!"

"You will deposit them in the files for the defense. We'll use them as evidence."

"She is considered worthy of every sacrifice, heroism and love. . . ."

She. That's how I have been taught to think of our legendary princess, since the days of my early youth. My beloved master, Rabbi Zur, of Bialystok, used to tell me often that in many folk tales and epic sagas humanity is represented as a woman, a princess served by noble knights and poor peasants alike. In Rabbi Zur's opinion, this was due to the fact that humanity is very demanding and even more difficult to satisfy. She is always in search of happiness and her innumerable lovers have devoted all their energy and genius to the task of satisfying her, and they often fought and killed and gave

92

up their own lives trying to fulfill her longing for a bliss that forever eludes her.

"Gardener," the Commissioner barks.

"Yes, sir. Anything you wish, as long as it's for Her Ladyship, sir."

"All with their asses bare?"

"*Jawohl*. All of them, sir. They all gave their best, sir. I only wish she'd let me try, too. I'm very good at it, sir. It runs in the family. My brother fought in the Second World War, my father gave his life in the First. I'm sure I'm as good as anyone, sir. But no, she gave it to everyone except me. Why? What's so repulsive about me? Why humiliate a son of the people? I have the same right to get killed as everybody else, this is a democracy!"

He leaves and I feel a bit sad. He is pure in heart, this good Johann. And he is right, too. She no longer counts on the elite, they had their chance and they failed miserably. Now she looks toward the little people, the masses. *Workers of all lands unite!* For quite a while she's been looking toward you hopefully. This is your chance, your golden opportunity. And who knows, there may even be some survivors.

15.

The Blinkers

They have been arguing for an hour. This is always the way when Lily's problems come up: words and swords, swords and words. The Baron even manages to find an interesting argument:

"Allow me, Commissioner. Let us be logical. As Lily could . . . entertain at home or in the park belonging to the castle, why should she suddenly dash off outside?"

"She has a taste for conquest."

"Lily? But she only dreams of peace!"

"That is the bloodiest dream of all, you ought to know that. In my turn, I am going to ask you to answer a question. How was it that, although you were surrounded by corpses—they were all over the park, according to your gardener—you noticed nothing?"

"I was not looking so low, Commissioner. I only had eyes for Lily. One saw only her. Her beauty is such that it hides everything else. A dazzling beauty, and you may find its reflection in all our museums. I loved her, I worshiped her. I did not regard her with a critical eye. I had unlimited faith in her."

"You must nevertheless have noticed that there was something that was not quite right? That she had . . . certain dark corners?"

"I beg your pardon!"

"Dark and nauseating corners, where odd things were happening."

"Commissioner, when you are a gentleman, there are certain dark corners where you do not look."

"You shut your eyes, eh?"

"I loved her. I did not watch her with skeptical, cynical, suspicious eyes."

"Corpses all over the place, and you saw nothing."

"It was hidden from us. We were kept in ignorance. We were fooled. Names like Auschwitz, Treblinka, we never heard them until after the war. We suspected that there had been some excesses, but we never knew the sordid details. And besides, I am still not convinced. A large part of it is propaganda."

"But it was all happening under your nose, in your own park! The evidence of your gardener, Johann, is conclusive. You could not walk on your own lawns, or dream in the moonlight, without treading on corpses!"

"My friend has already told you that he has never been mixed up in politics," the Count intervenes. "When you stumble on corpses, you know quite well that there is an ideological problem there, and you don't want to get mixed up in that, do you?"

"I believed that these corpses were just rumors, spread by the Communists," the Baron states firmly.

The Count's moustache droops sadly. "Dear, great, and unhappy friend!" he murmurs. "I have the horrible impression that this is worse than a nightmare: this is reality! Gone is the age of enlightenment . . . Rousseau! Voltaire! Diderot! True, they sometimes were cynical, but at least they had style! They knew how to speak of our beloved, with beautiful words worthy of her!"

"Of course, the bastards lived off her charms!"

95

"Cohn!"

The Baron pulls out his handkerchief, dabs his noble brow. Schatzchen and I are shaking with laughter, we have been the prey of so much *hilaris* only once before, he and I, in the month of August 1966, when a special session of the Congress of World Jewry was held in Brussels, on the possibility of talks between Jews and Germans. That was the best joke we had ever heard.

The two distinguished humanists observe the Chief of the Licht Police with dismay; their disgust and consternation can only be understood by people who, since the days of their first governess, have been brought up to venerate the Mona Lisa and have never seen anything else in her cynical smile except the perversity of all our cultural values and their reassuring prevalence over massacres, horror, and beastliness. For these two, one thing is clear: Lily has fallen prey to *reality*. Culture is assailed by truth: this is the end of idealism. The reason? Our princess of the legends, our madonna of the frescoes, has fallen into the hands of the people. Rascally democracy, without a trace of Leonardo or Goethe, is dragging their beloved, whose image has been so high on the walls of our cultural places of worship, down into the mud.

The Baron is so outraged that he even manages to recover a certain dignity. "Commissioner, your brutishness can no longer be tolerated. A very great and universally revered lady is in mortal peril, and this merely inspires in you uncontrollable giggles. I shall refer the matter to your superior, but meanwhile, I insist on immediate assistance!"

Schatz and I pull ourselves together.

Where were we?

Ah, yes, those beastly murders in the Forest of Geist. We were in the process of interrogating the witnesses.

Where are they, all those witnesses for the prosecution?

It's strange, but they are there, and screaming, those millions of witnesses, only because they are no longer there.

And who is conducting this inquiry, anyway? Schatzchen knows that he has moments of absence, when he is not entirely himself and not at all master of his thoughts. *Yeah, this is known as overkill.*

Who said that?

Always this accursed . . . *occupation,* the outrageous occupation of Germany by dead Jews has got to stop. Propaganda, that's what it is. Those damned dead're keeping the flame burning. Kill the bloody bastards! What the hell is von Thadden doing? *Deutschland erwache!*

I've got to pull myself together. What is needed here is a new drug, that would wipe out the memory and the dybbuks.

I feel a little better. He is fading a bit. I've suppressed him . . . *Allow me, Cohn, it is I who . . . Not at all, Schatzchen, I am in charge of this case. . . . Cohn, let go of me. . . . Come on, Schatzchen, come on . . .*

Rakhmones! Will it ever be possible to disentangle the Nazi from the Jew, the victim from the executioner, so deeply united in the very semen of the species?

16.

TFOU, TFOU, TFOU

I don't know if this is the effect of the German awakening, of the general rebirth of virility and national pride in the land, but for the last moments Schatzchen has been toying with a desperate idea and I find myself murmuring cautious advice to my host. What do they want, the Germans? To start all over again, only to be spat upon, and find themselves landed with two thousand years of guilt and hatred, thus giving birth, perhaps, to a new Christian civilization, *tfou, tfou, tfou?*

"Cohn, you don't understand. It's always been the German people's historical task. We've got a great mission to fulfill. We've got to muster all our strength once more and fuck her. happy this time, once and for all, because that's what the German *Seehnsucht* and *Weltschmerz* are about. Why do you think she keeps running amok? Because of frustration. She longs for the absolute fulfillment. We won't have peace on earth unless someone goes out there and fucks her real good, once and for all. Happiness, that's what she keeps looking for. We've got what it takes."

I plead with Schatzchen, I hold him back, I warn him to stay away from the *Nazional Partei Deutschland's* and to keep his reborn virility and that old German yearning under control. Enough is enough. The Germans have fucked her blue generation after generation, thirty million stiffs in their last effort, and nothing, she didn't make it. I don't think she'll ever make happiness, unless someone truly fucks her dead, and what kind of happiness is that?

"Listen, stupid, let the Americans try this time, or the Russians, or the Chinese, or let them all fuck her together. The Germans have done all they could."

"Cohn, we won't shrink from our German duty. We've got to go out there and give it to her real good."

"Shut up. Stop muttering. Can't you see we're being watched? We don't want to have another fit, do we?"

Just as I say these words, the door opens and Inspector Guth comes in.

"What about the press?"

We hesitate a little. But we feel it is better for us to be seen in full control of ourselves, conducting our inquest with a cool head and masterly hand. It will put an end once and for all to those invidious rumors being spread about by our enemies, about our sanity.

"Bring them in."

It is an onslaught. They come from all over the world, and they have only one thought in their heads: the German atrocities. Twenty years after the final solution, the London *Sunday Times* still has the *hutzpeh* to publish a color supplement on "Anti-Semitism in Germany." What anti-Semitism? There are only thirty thousand live Jews left in Germany; do you think something great can be built on a puny figure like that?

We have a moment of terror when the flash bulbs explode but we pull ourselves together: I cannot be seen where I am, inside.

I sulk a bit. I would like very much to be photographed. I never achieved real fame. I remained a third-rate entertainer all my life. I ought to have emigrated to America: over there, I might have become a new Groucho Marx.

The telephone keeps ringing.

"Hello, hello, yes?" we shout. "The League of the Rights of Man? Commissioner Cohn speaking. The League of the Rights of Man is indignant? Well, that's their job, isn't it? And anyhow, this is a democracy. What does that mean? It means *that the victims were all willing*. Look here, it is really not the fault of the police that she can't make it! Nothing is good enough. Socialism? She has already tried that. It went *psh-psh-psh*. . . . Everything's been tried. They've given it to her from every angle and in every position. What? You've got an idea? Go on. Yes . . . Yes, I'm listening. . . . What? But that's disgusting. I know she would try anything, even the Chinese . . . but THAT! Sir, you're a pig!"

We hang up the phone. The journalists are interested.

"What did he say?"

"He claims that he knows an infallible trick."

"What trick?"

"A trick."

"Commissioner, people are yearning for happiness and if someone has discovered a new trick, they have the right to know . . ."

"But I'm telling you, it's something really filthy!"

"Then it has a good chance of being successful. Commissioner, sir, in the name of the people, of the yearning multitudes, tell us the trick! You have no right to suppress ideas."

"But it's nothing but filth again, I'm telling you."

"Maybe this is the right kind!"

Schatz, who has been hearing strident, disembodied, dispossessed voices coming from all sides—a good dybbuk knows how to make himself heard from one end of the earth to the other, and I am told that there are even some Vietnamese kids who have learned the *shtik*—Schatz keeps grabbing the telephone with a shaking hand.

"Hello, hello, what? One million Chinese with their asses bare? And nothing? What do you mean, nothing? A million dead Chinese, it's still better than nothing. . . . Hello, what? The Ringling Brothers Circus? They have a suggestion to make? WHAT? To place some poisoned human flesh in her way? Sir, she's not a wild animal, she's a very great lady! Vietnam? What's Vietnam got to do with it? I'm telling you: a very noble family!"

THE BARON: "Goethe! Schiller! Lessing!"

THE COUNT: "Montaigne! Descartes! Pascal!"

ME: "All with their asses bare!"

SCHATZ: *"Gevalt!"*

ME (kissing him on the forehead): *"Bei mir bist du sheyn!"*

GOETHE: "Mehr Licht!"

DE GAULLE: "Princess of the legends . . . Madonna of the frescoes . . ."

NAPOLEON: (he goes psh-psh-psh . . .)

HITLER: (he goes psh-psh-psh . . .)

LORD RUSSELL: (he goes psh-psh-psh . . .)

ALBERT SCHWEITZER: (he goes psh-psh-psh . . .)

JESUS:

"Oh, no, not Him!" roars Schatz. "We, the Germans, we will never again allow anyone to touch the Jews!"

Shivers run down my spine. I suddenly feel that a new and terrible danger is threatening those of my race: *new Nazis who would not be anti-Semitic.* Just think of the terrible, irreparable harm that could be done to us by a new Hitler who was not at all against the Jews, who was only against the Chinese?

I feel faint. Suppose they make me an offer?

Tfou, tfou, tfou.

PART
TWO

IN THE
FOREST
OF
GEIST

17.

The Jewish Holes

They carried us away. The doctors called an ambulance, they gave us an injection, and they took us away on a stretcher. Almost immediately, I began to feel that Schatz was fading away and I started to rub my hands gleefully: in a moment or two, I shall be rid of him. It must be wonderful, for a Jew to feel de-Nazified at last. It's no life to be condemned to haunt the subconscious of your executioner.

You can't even call the place a subconscious: it is a garbage dump. No light, no air, darkness closing in on you from all sides, old Nazi slogans, still visible after all these years, stink and rot everywhere. You call that hospitality? Nobody comes to clean the place, on the contrary, every day someone throws in more filth. When it's not the neo-Nazis, it's all sorts of historical refuse: sickening, worn-out ideas of another age, vile stains of blood and of God knows what, still stirring and only asking to be of service again, obscene ideological props and, a moment ago, there fell on top of the heap, of all things, a salt shaker, a watering can, forty-one bare-assed stiffs, six pairs of socks and twelve volumes of the *Encyclopædia Britannica:* when it's not one thing, it's another.

So you may imagine how pleased I was when they stuck the needle in our arm. Almost immediately, we were seized with uncontrollable laughter: he was going ha-ha-ha! and I was going ho-ho-ho! and neither of us could stop. Everything would have gone off very well if one of the doctors hadn't blundered, saying to the other, with a note of professional satisfaction in his voice:

"It is really most effective in shock cases. The state of hilarity is infinitely stronger and more lasting than with laughing gas. . . ."

There are some words which you don't say twice to a Jew and the word "gas" is one of them. I was roaring with laughter, while at the same time conscious that something was happening, that I was fading away. But at the mention of the word "gas," my instinct of self-preservation came into play. Even while still giggling merrily, I summoned what strength I had left and began to kick so hard inside Schatz that my host sat up on the stretcher and began to yell:

"No! Once is enough! Leave the bastard alone! If you suppress him again, they'll start all that talk about genocide once more!"

Then he jumped off the stretcher and started running down the road like a rabbit. Naturally, I ran after him: I had been entrusted with a task by the German people and I am not one to shrink from duty. I didn't choose to be a dybbuk—it was the Germans who made that choice for me —but I am determined to do my best, as you may have noticed.

It was quite extraordinary that my buddy had the strength to run the way he did, considering the dose of Ennoctal they had pumped into us. As it happened, there was a parade of neo-Nazis marching through our town of Licht, screaming *Deutschland erwache,* singing *We shall march again* and *Let us get our beloved Fatherland back from the Poles,* and it must have boosted Schatz's morale considerably, because he gave von Thadden the Nazi salute, and even had the time to stop briefly on his way, open his fly, and show his thing proudly to the new Fuehrer, to prove that he had not yet been circumcised. The new Fuehrer showed him his, and as a tremendous cheer arose from all this marching, rising virility, I experienced a moment of optimism, of wild hope. You never can tell, maybe von Thadden and his neo-Nazis will make it, maybe Germany will go through it all again? I must confess that there are moments when I wish it for them from the bottom of my grave.

Schatz made it straight to the Forest of Geist—*Geist*, as you may know, in German means a happy mixture of the words "soul" and "spirit"—which has always been the favorite dwelling place of German *Kultur* and inspired some of the bloodiest massacres and destructions in history.

We crawled into some bushes and under some trees, and such was his state of utter moral and intellectual prostration that Schatz fell asleep almost at once, stretched out, mouth open and snoring, sheltered by the bushes. I cuddle by his side, take his hand, and gaze tenderly at my buddy. I caress his brow, chase the flies away, and try to keep it shipshape and pretty, ready for my return. His subconscious may be what it is, but we still call it home. And so, for a short half-hour or so, I let him be and drift around admiring our beautiful old Forest of Geist and smelling the flowers.

In the last forty-eight hours the Forest has been closely guarded by the police. It is forbidden to enter it without a special police permit.

I know the Forest well. I often walk up and down past the oak trees which led to the ruins of what was once an old house. A de luxe residence and a kindergarten have taken its place, but you can still see the graves which the SS made us dig before killing us. God knows for what future use they are kept, though officially they were labeled "shrines" and tourists often visit them. Mine is here, under that fir tree, at your service. There is no guide, but any kid from Licht will always offer to show you what they call here "the Jewish holes."

So, the Forest of Geist is one of my favorite spots and I often drag Schatzchen here. We sit under an oak, the two of us, listening, as a Yiddish poet wrote, to "the sobbing of the violins of autumn"—autumn 1943, to be precise—and on a fine day you can hear the sobs rising from the German earth, however little ear you may have. I have seen my buddy spend hours beside the hole which he once made me dig; he keeps looking down, where the grass is so thick. Once he did a rather extraordinary thing. Suddenly, he jumped right into the hole . . . and you know what he did? *He lay down at the bottom, waiting.* Strange, wasn't it? I didn't understand that gesture at all, and I still don't understand it. He was stretched out on his back, his face white, his eyes wide open. I felt rather annoyed. What the hell, it was my place. I had paid quite a price for the right to lie there. If he thought someone would grab a Schmeisser and machine-gun him, so that he could pay and be left in peace at last, he was sadly mistaken. There are other ways of getting even.

Anyway, he remained motionless at the bottom of the hole, clutching tufts of Jewish grass in his hands. I felt rather embarrassed by this offer, by these suddenly reversed roles. I could do nothing for him: there was nobody to shout *Fire!* and I had no machine gun. In any case, I wouldn't have killed him, even if I could. Sometimes I wonder if I am not a bit cruel.

What I do know, though, is why he has dragged me into the Forest of Geist once again. It's Lily who draws him there, of course. He loved his wife very much, who was also named Lily—I can assure you that she was very beautiful— but after three years of marriage she left him, on the pretext that she didn't want to share her husband with another person. She had become very neurotic. She told everyone that her husband always dragged a Jew around with him, and that she had had enough of it. She had nothing against Jews, but all the same there were some places and some moments when they had no business showing up suddenly, it was disgusting. At the time, everyone thought the girl was nuts; there was a divorce. I remember that my friend Schatz threw a fit when I expressed the polite hope that the court would give him, and not his wife, the custody of their Jew. I can't even make a joke any longer. That son of a bitch takes everything too seriously.

18.

The Princess
of the Legends,
the Madonna
of the Frescoes

I wander a little at random. I know that Florian spends his
time in the Forest of Geist: he loves to walk there. By the
way, I often wonder how he came by his name, Florian. All
I know is that in an old sixteenth-century fairy tale I used
to read when I was a kid there was a drawing of Death
walking in a woods and the artist's name, I remember quite
well, was Florian. Anyway, Florian comes here to dream, to
meditate, and to harvest. He is very keen on meditation: he
has a rather philosophical turn of mind, something that is
probably due to his rather special relationship with life.

There are pretty streams here, which burble over the
pebbles, as they should. Ferns. Little birds. Cheep-cheep and
tweet-tweet from every branch. Butterflies all over the place,
fragile and ephemeral. There are no eagles: we are too low
down. There are no wolves either, no Red Ridinghoods, and
no grandmothers. History has taken care of the fairy tales,
our forest has been touched by a certain realism, it has lost
its smell of childishness and innocence. On Sundays, you
will find lovers there, because of the Jewish holes. They are
very convenient for lovemaking.

I emerge into a clearing. There are some ruins here, not very interesting ones, stones blackened by ancient fires, nothing very poetical, nothing particularly inspired, strictly routine. Some rocks too, and in the distance a very pretty view, with a castle. I suddenly notice a few books, balanced on a rock. I can't help smiling. Lily and Florian always leave a lot of literature behind them.

I was not mistaken. I have barely noticed the books, when Florian emerges upon the landscape. He holds a knife in his hand and he is wiping it carefully. He whistles a little tune that sends a chill down your spine, that is, if you've got a spine.

I notice at once that slight infirmity with which he is afflicted: those pretty yellow butterflies which flutter so charmingly fall dead when he passes by. It is an absolutely natural phenomenon and he can do nothing about it. I am not even certain if he is aware of it. He sits down on a stone, takes a sausage out of his pocket, and starts cutting it into thin slices, very neatly. He eats. I don't know why he reminds me of Mack the Knife, in the *Threepenny Opera*. Maybe it's his way of dressing. A checked suit, very loud, a black shirt, a white tie; on his tie he wears a pin, which looks very strange with those clothes: it is a gold cross with a little Christ nailed onto it. A trophy, sort of. It was his first trophy, and he is still proud of it. We all guard a certain affection for the honors which we received at our beginnings.

He looks striking, old Florian. A bony face, flat, and the skin only seems to be there out of respect for the conventions. The eyes are without light, the lids without lashes. Not one wrinkle. It is a face rather like that of a tortoise, slightly prehistoric. It is not unattractive, nevertheless. A certain lack of expression, of course, a fixed, bleak look. One guesses that life has overwhelmed him, and has already given him everything which it had to offer.

I suddenly feel my heart beating very loudly. I can't help it: I have always been a great sentimentalist. And, once again, my position is so delicate, so confused too, that when I say "I" it is impossible for me to be sure who, exactly, is speaking. That's the trouble with a moral conscience, with the subconscious and with certain interesting historical conditions. It can be me, it can be Schatzchen, or even you—and by "you," I mean Your Most Illustrious Highness of the Western World, heir to the greatest civilization the world has ever seen, the strangest characteristic of the dybbuk, that real scum of our sewers, being that he has an almost endemic tendency to nose into all our most exalted places. Your Highness will excuse me, it is my immanent, immaterial, and omnipresent nature which drives me ceaselessly to recognize myself in Her, a mere stain, a speck of dust, a tiny drop of fly-shit. Let us talk about Jung and the collective subconscious and let it go at that. So, my heart is up to its old tricks again, and a smile of wonder comes to my lips: I watch our beloved, our princess of the legends, the madonna of the frescoes, appear once more, pure, lovely, and divine, among our charred bones and ruins. I can almost see Lord Russell, Albert Schweitzer, and Albert Camus holding her train. At the same instant a waterfall throws itself at her feet, peacocks take up their positions on the branches of the trees, looking like Persian miniatures, Raphael cherubs begin to rustle around her, unicorns are gamboling, Dürer springs forward hat in hand, kneels down and awaits her orders. Donizetti breaks loose, Watteau takes care of her smile, Hans Holbein the Younger throws his murdered Christ at her feet to give her the look of the Virgin, and at once hundreds of our greatest Christs arrange themselves picturesquely around for the satisfaction of the eye. I recognize the Christ of Jörg Ratbeg with a yellow and blue world painted as a background for His head, another one on the left by Grünewald, covered with thorns and in the process of being flagellated, but I hardly have time to smile with aesthetic delight—the *Decapitation of Saint John the Baptist* particularly enchants me—when it all changes and fades away, the Renaissance takes over and Italian painting gives our beloved an even more dazzling setting. In short, all the art of centuries leaps into the scales and reestablishes instantly the balance, in spite of the hundreds of millions of her exterminated lovers: there is no more deficit, Our Lady is so surrounded by beauty that the blood and tears are instantly covered up with immortal art by her servants, she regains her virginity, the most terrible crimes turn into mines of precious gems, of themes, of sources of inspiration, into fountains out of which the Beauty gushes, each new horror acting as a galvanization of our creative genius. Tiepolo drapes a gay sky over her in his own manner, sheep, shepherds, and ruins work together toward a happy Hubert Robert effect, a lute descends within reach of her hand, Fragonard looks after her complexion, Renoir works on her sweet little ear, Bonnard on her tiny foot, Velázquez on her royal bearing, she is accompanied wherever she goes by her makeup artists and her heroic and inspiring historical tapestry.

Suddenly, I am aware that I am making a mistake which Rabbi Zur, of Bialystok, my beloved master, had frequently cautioned me about: *I am looking her full in the face.* I was only twelve and it was the evening before *Bar Mitzvah* when Rabbi Zur, who wanted to make me into a worthy and idealistic man, taught me one of the rules of life from which, in his opinion, I should never depart. Moshele, he told me, you must never, under any excuse or in any circumstance, look at humanity too closely or too carefully. I wanted to know why. The holy man seemed embarrassed. It dazzles you, he ended by explaining to me. You see, Moshele, humanity is so beautiful that we must be content to love her and to serve her without ever examining her lovely nature with too careful an eye. Otherwise, you risk losing your sight or even your mind. Thus, for example, it is thanks to this faithfully observed rule that the Jews have survived, in spite of everything, and have not gone mad. Whenever humanity manifested herself too crudely around them, they averted their eyes. It was not cowardice, but merely a certain tact and prudence. And that's why, Moshele, we can still find great humanists and true lovers of the human breed among us Jews. *Mazel tov.*

Rabbi Zur of Bialystok even told me a much greater secret.

An oral tradition exists according to which Jesus, before being killed, insisted on observing this same Hebraic rule. *He is supposed to have asked to be blindfolded.* It was hard to have shown a greater sign of pity and love toward humanity. It was the most beautiful gesture of tact and *savoir-faire* of all time.

Rabbi Zur had meditated a great deal about this and he had come to a conclusion: *The Messiah, when he comes, will be a blind man.*

I must confess that, since my adventure, I have become rather careless and even foolhardy in this respect. I have nothing to lose. I feel that I have learned all there is to learn about our legendary princess.

So I look at her to my heart's content. Features of such purity, such delicacy . . . an adorable little nose, a tender and appealing mouth, which has emerged immaculate from all its encounters. And what an air of innocence, what a look of modesty, of vulnerability! When one thinks that she has barely lowered her skirt after her last effort, one can but bow in awe before the genius of her faithful servants who have already had time to redecorate her from head to foot. I think I can even see Titian and all the *quattrocento* brigade hiding in the bushes, with their makeup kits, but it must be nerves with me.

She sits down beside Florian, who is still sausaging. Watching him eat gives one a weird sensation. I would have thought that he had had his bellyful a long time ago. There is something dreamlike about his presence, his very reality confers a character of fantasy upon him. Is it perhaps my Jewish spitefulness which gives an Eichmannite quality of banality to what is pompously called "the tragic grandeur of Death"? More likely it's the sausage, the greasy paper, and the knife. It looks vulgar, and is probably an effort to preserve his incognito. He knows that if people could meet Death in person they would rush to ask for favors, they are irresistibly attracted by power. Florian has had quite enough of the chores which go hand in hand with fame. He loves anonymity and succeeds admirably in passing unnoticed: he has learned to hide his presence in statistics.

He wipes his knife and tucks it away under his belt, throwing the greasy paper behind the rock, like any other picnicker. Now he takes a lipstick and powder box out of his pocket and hands them to Lily. She carefully removes the marks left by her latest love encounter. I suddenly have the feeling that I am taking part in some great artistic activity of the world. Museums are once more overflowing with treasures, there is a retrospective exhibition of eight hundred Picassos, another one of Vermeer, the Louvre stays open even at night, German towns buy masterpieces at any price and wallow in beauty, the city of Düsseldorf even goes as far as to acquire the portrait of the exterminated Jewish poet Max Jacob by the Jew Modigliani, and hangs it on its walls: Germany redeems itself.

"Who was that gentleman, Florian?"

What a voice! Quite simply, it's not a voice, it's pure Mozart.

A kind of smile passes across his face, over which everything merely passes.

"A small-timer."

Florian also has a very beautiful voice, deep, rather sepulchral, but fascinating, fascinating.

"Just another small-timer, my darling. There was no need for you to bother. I've told you a million times: they can't deliver. They don't have what it takes. Eunuchs, all of them."

Something really odd is happening to me. I don't know whether it's her voice, or that disturbing warmth which oozes from her, but I sense that I am beginning to emerge from my abstract state. For I need hardly tell you that there is nothing allegoric about Lily: she is a creature of our flesh and of our blood. She's got what it takes, no doubt about that. The effect is, as usual, galvanizing. You are seized by a violent longing to accomplish something. You feel in a monumental frame of mind, you look at the proudest oak trees as equal to equal. It is one of those moments of absolute certainty when man really measures up to his dreams of conquest and ceases to doubt his own greatness. This time, you are going to fuck her happy, you are sure of your own strength, of your powers, of your system, it's no longer mere idealism, at last you are grasping something solid. You draw yourself up to your full height, you put yourself into position, you unfurl your ideological banner, you thrust it forward, and you set yourself to work on the construction of socialism. But Lily dreams of a happiness which is entirely beyond her reach and entirely beyond your means, no matter how impressive they may be. Your flame and ardors end up exactly as have those of all the other resolute lovers who have fucked themselves dead before you. She lets you do your trick, she still presses you tenderly in her arms, but her nostalgic glance is already seeking a new man of destiny. Your eyes start to bulge out of your head, your tongue hangs out, your back is breaking, you try to do your best, but you know you are going to lose your foothold at any moment, you muster up all your ideological resources, you try to make History, you are up to some unheard-of filthy tricks, you find yourself in positions whose existence you hadn't even suspected. From trick to trick, you suddenly land in Vietnam and you are ready to try something even filthier when you realize that she is already looking over your shoulder and smiling at someone who is waiting his turn behind you. You clench your teeth, you call for help, you yell "Workers of the world, unite!" but at the very moment when, half suffocated, your mouth full of God knows what, completely outraged by her demands, and reduced to your simplest expression, you are only hanging on by a thread, you suddenly hear her voice murmuring ironically to you:

"And with your ears, darling, don't you do any nice tricks?"

You collapse. You let out a terrible scream, you become sadistic, you kill, you burn, you torture, but she has already tested all human powers to the full, she doesn't even notice that anymore. What you need to fuck her truly happy is the absolute weapon, and for that you've got to equip your striking force with the nuclear warhead, but let me tell you that you will not succeed in satisfying her with a mere prosthesis. It is then that the oldest ideological argument in the world starts all over again, the question of whether she is frigid or you are impotent, and there is no way of proving your virility to her except by giving it to her once and for all, which is known as a crime of passion. In fact, what she really needs is a supreme sally by God himself. But I'll tell you something, between you and me, in the greatest secrecy: God is not a man.

Ssh.

19.

A Perfect Couple

All the same, I hopefully raise my eyes toward the blue sky: but no, nothing, there is no sign. Immensity is there all right, but it does not take the necessary shape. It is in vain that Lily's glance wanders dreamily through the infinite. However, the Talmud does say that Divine Power rises, that it does not descend, that it goes up and never falls down: according to the *Cabala*, it is an "upwards" and not a "downwards," a point of view shared by Teilhard de Chardin, and that is why only the celestial spheres can be seen from the earth. According to the *Mahābhārata*, in order to be fulfilled, Humanity should rise above the love-god, in the position that Krishna makes her assume in certain sculptures in the temples of Nepal. I fear, however, that Lily is condemned to yearning. It is in vain that, in the second parable, Eleazar ben Zohai speaks of the "terrestrial Cow fulfilled by the celestial Bull." It is nothing but a pious hope.

She leans against a rock, raises her eyes to heaven, and waits. I would not wish to sound disrespectful toward such a great lady, but one really must say that she looks rather like a whore soliciting. Those wonderful eyes are not without a certain languorous suggestiveness. She passes her hands over her hips, over her breasts, and waits, her eyes raised toward the Almighty. . . .

Tfou, tfou, tfou.

It is then that I notice, here and there on the grass, a dozen or so pairs of carefully folded pants, and a few pairs of shoes. Not bad for a Monday. There is something humble and pathetic about these so clearly expressed human limitations, when faced with the immensity of the sky. I feel that the Almighty ought not to insist with such satisfaction on our size. I have even come to wonder whether this rather heavy insistence is not a proof that He has some secret doubt. Lily's yearning is of such magnitude that heaven must be questioning itself rather nervously about its own resources.

She sighs. Florian, who is sharpening a piece of wood with his knife, shakes his head.

"Come on, luv. You mustn't be discouraged. There is a train to Hamburg at four o'clock. Dr. Klaps is waiting for us. He is the greatest since Freud, everyone agrees on that. He's worked real miracles, and he mentions some of them in his book, *The Enchanted Soul*. Remember the banker's wife who could only reach happiness when she heard the cashbox bell ringing, which put her in an impossible situation since it always woke up her husband? Dr. Klaps solved her problem, luv. And the little woman who could only reach the heights from the window of the Ritz in Paris, while looking at the Vendôme column? Dr. Klaps restored her to simplicity, peach. She no longer needs monuments, she is content with what is on hand. And the Countess who could only reach perfection in a traffic jam? And the other one who could only make it in the arms of jockeys weighing exactly one hundred and ten pounds? Today, they have become simple, honest women, luv, Dr. Klaps has found a cure for all these deep problems of their immortal souls. He'll solve your case in no time at all."

"Do you really think so?"

"I am sure of it, peach. Psychoanalysis has an answer to everything. It will free the human soul from those abysses, from those unbelievable depths in which it flounders. Remember the woman whose husband, before presenting himself, had to offer bread and salt as well as an extremely rare Afghanistan stamp, having first moved all the furniture around? And the little chemist's wife from Berne who had to be encouraged by a roaring lion? And the other one, whose husband had to imitate the noise of a jet plane? Dreaming humanity, unfathomable mysteries of the soul, what hidden treasures, what diversity! Today, they have all become respectable, easily gratified women, peach. Dr. Klaps is certainly the greatest since Dr. Marx. They will put an end to your suffering, peach, I am convinced of that."

Lily seems reassured. She takes off her straw hat and throws it onto the grass. Her fair hair appears in all its radiance. She is wearing a charming, thin summer dress with yellow flowers on it, and sandals. She shuts her eyes and offers her face to the sun.

Florian has pushed his felt hat back on his head. He has picked up a book and, leaning with his elbows on his knees, he turns the pages. How strange: they have assumed exactly the attitude they had in the painting by an unknown artist which used to hang on the wall in our living room when I was a child: *Death Reading to Humanity the History of Her Crimes*. I was six years old when I began asking my father questions about the painting and my father always tactfully eluded a straight answer. "It's an allegory." That was all he would tell me, but then one day he went on business to Berdichev and the Cossacks of Petlyura killed him and the painting ceased to look merely allegorical to me.

A kind of lightness and gaiety surrounds the couple, as though nature itself were endeavoring to please her oldest companions.

Insects and birds continue to fall at Florian's feet. Lily looks at the poor, multicolored heap which by now reaches

Florian's knees—I can almost see Socrates, Goethe, and Napoleon among them—and frowns.

"Stop that, Florian, it's disgusting."

The remark clearly upsets him. His face turns pale. I think she has touched on a sensitive point.

"You know perfectly well I can't help it," he says rather emphatically. "Do you really think it's pleasant for me to kill flies? For me the death of Einstein, of Abraham Lincoln, of Mozart? We all have our little infirmities."

Lily sighs. She is looking at all the empty trousers on the grass, the empty shoes.

"Florian?"

"Yes, luv?"

"Who was the heroic little soldier with the stupid face?"

"How should I know? Just one other heroic little soldier with a stupid face."

"You don't kill a young man, Florian, without looking afterwards to see who you have killed. That's known as manners!"

Florian's voice takes on a cynical note, and his smile reappears. "My peach, an old professional like me has none of that curiosity left. I haven't taken the slightest interest in their faces for a long time. They want to give you happiness, all right, I let them show what they can do. I let them try. . . . They fail. They must be punished for their incredible presumption. I am not going to lean tenderly over each gnat who has visions of greatness and power, and who breaks down on the way. They only upset you."

But Lily disapproves. She cares about style, and manners. She is shocked. "Still, you should have made a note of his name. You always do that with heroes."

"If and when there appears among your admirers a great lover with a new system, and if he finds a way of solving your problems, we'll record his name for posterity, peach.

We will make him famous. We will put his . . . well, his head on a new series of stamps, and the rest will be sung by our greatest poets and historians. Meanwhile, I am not going to take note of every bit of straw. They fail you. I knock them down. It's History."

I am painfully aware of the vulgarity of Florian's voice: one feels oneself in the presence of boundless Cynicism, and only the slight smell of garlic sausage gives him something human. I consider this coarseness inexcusable in the presence of such a great lady. After all, Florian's is the oldest profession in the world, and one from which we derive all our tragic character.

Lily shakes her marvelous hair, which haloes her head with all the gold of Florence. "They are so terribly limited, all of them! And what vulgarity! Their love scenes remind me of a customs inspection, one emerges from their arms as though from a police search, all their famous skill of which they are so proud is just that of a pickpocket: I never notice anything."

"That's known as reality, luv. You must avoid it at all costs. Dreams are the only things that truly matter. There is no such thing as a frigid woman, there are only women who know how to dream and men who have nothing to offer them but their . . . reality, peach."

She smiles. But that is not the right word for this staggering phenomenon. The entire Forest of Geist lights up and is transformed before my eyes into a battlefield covered with inspired corpses.

"I know how to dream, Florian."

"And how, luv. Nobody has any doubt about that. You have proved it. That is why young men fall down around you like flies. They are dealing with a dream of perfection, peach. It does not forgive."

20.

Inside

I hold my breath. I am hidden by the bushes, she can't see me and, anyhow, in my present condition, what do I risk? She has had me.

But I know myself. And I am afraid of my own eyes: they are those of a lover. I am incorrigible. I believe that I can still be of use. I almost feel myself being reborn, *tfou, tfou, tfou*. Resurrection, I wouldn't wish that on my best friend.

Someone grabs my arm. I let out a yell, jump aside: maybe it's the Messiah, let's beat it while there's still time. But not at all. It's only Schatz. His face is grayish, his body shakes, he can hardly keep on his feet.

"Cohn, don't you feel something funny?"

In fact, yes. I do feel something. It is not exactly persecution, but I certainly have the impression that someone is trying to get rid of me. And not only of me. Of Germany, of the six million dead Jews, of Auschwitz, of humanity, of History, and of our bloody Forest of Geist itself. A kind of desperate wish for a total break with our very nature, of total rejection, of some kind of absolute disgust and vomit. It's enough to make one believe there is a man there who is trying to get rid of me, of Schatz, of History, to free himself from the very species to which we all belong and this, by some means the nature of which I still cannot guess, which smacks of some cowardly trick, of some kind of self-therapy. An artist, probably a writer, tfou, tfou, tfou. If I were a believer, I would say it was God trying to create the world at last, an idea which has not yet occurred to Him, unless you consider this world to be a creation, an insult which would not even spring to the mind of an atheist.

I am suddenly seized with such funk that I am not even sure they want to eliminate us from their conscience. It may be something even more dastardly. They may be trying to resuscitate me and put me back into my skin for some future use, a new persecution.

I'm getting gooseflesh, which is already in itself extremely alarming. Gooseflesh is a characteristic sign of being alive. Something revolting is going on, but what? A reconciliation between Germans and Jews? No, not that, all horror has its limits.

The thought occurs to me that thousands of artists have made works of great beauty out of the suffering of Christ. They have feasted on it. I also remember that out of mutilated corpses of Guernica Picasso produced *Guernica,* and Tolstoy milked war and peace for his *War and Peace.* I've always believed that if we still talk about Auschwitz and Treblinka, it's because the thing has not yet been redeemed by a beautiful work of literature.

Am I, by any chance, being written up, or turned into a work of art or a poem, God forbid? That's one way of getting rid of me, a well-known method of exorcising the dybbuk.

One thing is certain: the same threat hangs over me and Schatz. You've only got to look at his face. He is terrified. I try to think calmly. I don't believe Lily has anything to do with it. She has already had me. In any case, in my present state the only thing I could offer her is spiritual consolation.

Schatz grabs my arm. I yell.

"Let go of me, you bastard. We're not allowed to touch pig."

"Cohn, this is not the moment to squabble. There's a guy here who is trying to get rid of us."

"What guy? Where?"

"We can't see him. We're *inside*."

"What are you talking about? Another little attack?"

"Cohn, I've been psychoanalyzed for the last twenty years. I know what I'm talking about."

"You think I don't know about your dirty little efforts *to get rid of me* . . ."

I swallow hard. For God's sake. He's right. There is a guy here who is trying to shake us both off. For years, probably, he has been living with the horror of Auschwitz and Treblinka in his heart, and now he has decided that he can't go on like this, that he has to get rid of the Nazi and the Jew once and for all. Schatz looks at me. "You understand now, huh?"

"Why? Why would he try to get rid of us?"

"Probably to make room for the Negroes or the Vietnamese. They're the thing now."

I glance around me. The Forest of Geist is still bathed in light, but that could be ironical. Lily is still half lying on the rocks, just as Humanity did in my father's painting, and Florian is sitting near her, reading a murder story. I hear the sound of the hunting horn, very far away. The horn, though invisible, is the only suspect element in all this. A phallic symbol?

"Cohn, we have landed in the subconscious of a sex maniac."

I try to remain calm. Everything is possible, in this world which is waiting to be created. All sorts of disgraceful and bogus little creations may well be in progress in the shadows.

But the thought that I have perhaps become a mere psy-choanalytical element is intolerable to me. However, the more I breathe the air around me, the more I notice that it stinks, and the worse it stinks the more likely it is that we are really dealing with a subconscious. Besides, guilt, Jews, Nazis, Death, Humanity, impotence, frigidity, the celestial bull—you don't have to be a genius to guess that we are dealing with an intellectual.

"He is trying to vomit us," Schatz mutters. "If he gets rid of us, Cohn, we'll cease to exist and to matter. We'll matter as little as all the other victims of History."

Plaintive whistling noises come from his nose. It's typical. Little does it matter to him where, how, in what, with whom, provided that he can exist.

"I can understand that he might want to vomit a Nazi of your sort," I say, "but what about me?"

"In his mind, we are associated forever," says Schatz. "It's only natural."

The monstrosity of this is such that I am seized by fits of laughter. The idea that the word "Jew" can correspond to the word "German" till the end of time, by a *natural* process of association, is a real apotheosis of humanity.

I take a deep breath and then, before the eyes of the be-wildered Schatz, I start to dance. One-two-three! And one-two-three! I don't know who that guy is and how I got into his subconscious together with that Nazi louse, but I do know how to dance our old *hora*, and I beg you to believe that my boots hit hard, I give him the works, I hope it hurts. With a bit of luck I shall succeed in giving him a new traumatic shock, the son of a bitch. The subconscious, that's what it's made for: traumatic shocks.

"Are you nuts, you?" yells Schatz. "A fine time for danc-ing!"

"I'm not dancing," I tell him. *"I'm trampling."*

And one-two-three! I start in again. After a while I feel better and I would very much like to know how *he* feels. It can't be too good. The proof is that I am not at all frightened anymore. My confidence has returned. I am here to stay. He is not going to get rid of me. It's not that I enjoy being there, in his shit of subconscious, but where else can I go? I'm just as badly off here as anywhere else. It's always the same shit of a subconscious everywhere. It's collective.

There is one thing which I did not foresee: Schatz is actually beginning to look better. It seems that in defending myself against expulsion, I was defending him too, in spite of myself. He takes a Volksdeutsche out of his pocket, stretches himself out on the grass, and smokes. He looks at me ironically.

"Thank you, Cohn," he says. "You saved me. Nothing can ever separate us, old man."

For a moment, I remain speechless, the full horror of my situation becoming quite clear to me. Are the victim and the executioner really condemned to remain bound to each other for as long as there will be men?

Perhaps I really should let myself be kicked out of that man's psyche, accept disappearance, dissolve myself completely in the collective Ocean which is or is not fraternal, but which at least allows you to drown yourself. Okay, but that guy has got to make an effort which is worthy of me. He must bleed, he must tear me out of himself with a shred of flesh. I hope he has enough talent. I would have liked a bit of genius, but it doesn't exist, or else the world would have been created long ago.

Meanwhile, I get back to Lily. One always goes back to her. Can you tell me the name of a single man who has managed to free himself of his bond with her and become truly inhuman? There is no such thing as an inhuman man, only God could claim such greatness.

21.

The Billy Goat

Whereupon I remember that it is already 1967 and that Lily has not yet been fulfilled, which leaves us very little time, if you think of the resentment and spite which she inspired in all those who have disappointed her and who are openly getting ready to suppress this compromising evidence of their inadequacy. I wish I could help her to reach happiness and I try to remember everything I once learned from Rabbi Zur of Bialystok about the *khokhme* and the *Cabala* and about some of the sayings of our Wise Men which could perhaps help her to achieve happiness. I think I've got an idea. This advice is not to be found in the Book, it was Rabbi Zur himself who thought of it. One day, a poor woodcutter named Motele came to see him.

"*Rebe,*" he said, "I can't go on any longer. I've got a cantankerous wife, eleven children, three aunts, a mother-in-law worth ten of them, and our poverty is such that we are all obliged to live in a single room. I can't bear this life anymore. If you can't find a solution, I shall hang myself."

Rabbi Zur thought for a long time. "Very well," said he, "I shall suggest a cure for you. You will get a goat, and you will make him live with you in your one room."

"*Rakhmones!*" cried the unhappy man. "Rabbi Zur has gone mad! Look here, I share this accursed room with a cantankerous wife, eleven children, three aunts, and a mother-in-law like twenty of them, and you want me to put a goat in there as well? You *mishugeh?*"

"Do what I tell you."

At Bialystok, one always obeyed Rabbi Zur. He was famous because of all the follies he had committed during his life and which had enabled him to attain wisdom. Motele obeyed. But every day he came and implored the *rebe:*

"That goat is driving me mad!" he wailed. "It pisses everywhere, it smashes everything, it stinks. I can't bear it any longer!"

This went on for two weeks and finally Motele rushed into Rabbi Zur's house tearing his hair.

"I am going to hang myself! I will not live another day with that goat! Do something!"

Rabbi Zur thought for a long time. "Well," he said at last, "throw the goat out of the house, that's it."

Motele threw the goat out and lived happily ever after, grateful to Rabbi Zur until his dying day.

The more I think about the goat, the more it seems to me that there lies the possible solution to Lily's problem. I am convinced that Rabbi Zur would have advised her to try it. It is true that she may have already done so, as this age does not lack stinking goats, thank God, and from Stalin to Hitler the beast has already left many people feeling happy, after they got rid of it.

I am about to suggest this expedient to Lily, when I hear the branches crackling: someone is coming, breathing noisily. I wonder for a moment whether it is not a wild boar, and why not? In Lily's desperate situation, she is not likely to overlook anything. But the branches part and I see the crimson face of Grüber, the cop from our traffic squad in Licht, and an active member of *Nazional Partei Deutschland's.* He holds a big revolver in his hand. This dimwit of a hero has come here to make a sensational capture, to put the handcuffs on the greatest pair of criminals of all time, to cover himself with glory from head to foot. He emerges from the bushes and looks at Lily, the revolver pointing in her direction. He has his finger on the trigger and he is so scared that he is shaking all over, he is perfectly capable of firing, he cannot contain himself any longer. I try to get up, but only manage to sink further into a soggy and malodorous miasma which was not there a moment ago. I try to extricate myself from this shit-heap but only succeed in getting more bogged down. There is no longer any doubt whatever, Schatz is right, we certainly are caught in the subconscious of a particularly vicious individual, and one who doesn't even know what he wants: sometimes he tries to get rid of me, sometimes he holds me back. An intellectual, manifestly, as with him sometimes it's the absolute, sometimes it's the police, God, humanity, Death, a salt shaker, the *Encyclopædia Britannica,* a watering can with a twisted spout. I try to yell, to give the alarm, that half-wit Grüber doesn't know who Lily really is, an old and illustrious family which goes back for a hundred thousand years: you can't strike her down like that without even having satisfied her, especially on German territory and right in the Forest of Geist, they will say again that the Germans have not changed, that they are always ready to begin again. I realize almost at once that Lily is in no danger at all. It's true that the overexcited Grüber is ready to pull the trigger, but he is shaking so hard that he is sure to miss. Lily looks at his weapon and smiles. The revolver appears to interest her keenly. It seems to be giving her new hope, she is regaining confidence. She runs a hand through her hair coquettishly, and I do not wish to be lacking in respect toward her but I must say that in spite of her stunning beauty and all that brilliance with which she is haloed—they knew how to paint light, those Renaissance guys—she really does look like a whore soliciting. I am pained. Once our masterpieces leave the museums, God knows where and in what state they will be when we get them back.

"Hello," she murmurs invitingly.

"In the name—of—the law," stammers Grüber the cop.

"Oh Florian, look. . . . How well armed he is!"

Florian sighs wearily. "We have already tried the police, luv. They didn't make it, did they?"

Lily pouts. "They didn't know how to set about it."

"The Gestapo, luv? You're being unfair."

"Florian, I simply *adore* the police . . ." She casts a languorous look at Grüber the cop. ". . . when it really knows how to go about it!"

"In the name of—of—the law!" stammers the victim in a rather raucous voice.

"Oh yes!"

"But you have already tasted it a thousand times, luv," says Florian with a trace of impatience. "I don't know what you can still be expecting from the police, really. It didn't solve your problems, luv. Do remember, you were even more unhappy than before."

"Be quiet, Florian. You don't believe in anything anymore. The police are so hard, so direct, so efficient!"

"The army isn't bad, either, luv."

". . . It is so simple . . . so brutal!"

She unfastens her belt. "Florian, the police have an answer to everything."

"I—I—I," sobs the representative of law and order.

He is still hugging his weapon, hugging it with both hands, but he is fascinated, dazzled, unable to resist her advances any longer, such a great lady, just think, surrounded by such a legend, people have told him so much about her, in every way, since his schooldays, he even went to the Munich picture gallery to see her, Dürer, Goethe at Weimar, the most beautiful castles in the world, he is going to get fixed, that swine, it's hereditary with him, Grandfather got fixed in '14–'18, Daddy got fixed at Stalingrad, but they were on the wrong side, it wasn't the right one, they didn't succeed because they were badly led, this time they will make it, the NPD is sure of itself. . . . Grüber the Party member takes another step forward.

A strong smell of goat penetrates the Forest of Geist. Grüber the cop has only one vote, but he is prepared to throw it into the ballot box, to live dangerously. He has regained the spirit of adventure, the taste for risk. *Deutschland erwache.* Lily smiles sweetly at him, I can see that where her robe of beauty almost touches the ground her little foot taps impatiently.

"Florian, do look at that inspired air, those hands ready to grab, that finger ready poised on the trigger . . . he aims so well! I know he won't miss."

"I–I–I–"

Schatz tries to stop him, but I don't know why, I stand up in front of him, and he hurriedly retreats. He looks at me, blinking with bewilderment, he doesn't understand. In fact, I do not understand myself. I am beginning to wonder whether, in the depths of his subconscious, that fellow whom I don't know, but whom I obviously haunt, does not secretly want Germany to become Nazi again. Didn't I myself welcome the news of the neo-Nazis' successes in Bavaria and in Hesse with a little smile of satisfaction? I didn't think I was so vindictive. I sometimes get the impression that Hitler did us even more harm than I would have thought possible.

The young German is clearly in a state of grace: the little absolute is there, within a hand's reach, it smiles at him, all it needs is a new resolute step forward in the old direction.

"I–I–"

"All right," says Florian. "There's a grotto over there. But I advise you to think carefully, young man, before following in

133

the footsteps of your ancestors. I hope that you are sure of your capabilities. Madame has a horror of being disappointed. She has a taste which is very difficult to satisfy: the taste for perfection. If you show yourself unworthy . . ."

He has a very acute sense of our possibilities, Florian. I have a certain affection for him. We have always been on good terms, he and I, based on reciprocal understanding and respect. Florian is all for equality. My uncle, Anatole Cohen, of Lodz, who died in his bed, greatly astonished me because he began to laugh in his last moments. I asked him what was the matter with him. "My children, when I think that I, a poor, uneducated Jew, am about to suffer the same fate as Julius Caesar!" That's Florian all over, that equality he grants you at the finish line.

I manage at last to take my worried eye from the young German, and I see that Lily has disappeared into the bushes.

Young Grüber, the Party member, seems all of a sudden hesitant about going in there and trying to succeed where his elders had failed so miserably, which only goes to show that the cynicism of the last twenty years, the lack of an ideal and the iconoclastic propaganda of decadent writers like Günter Grass left their mark.

"Go on, do your best!" Florian encourages him. "I know you will make her happy. She is looking for a man of destiny! Son, you will make the whole world resound with the echo of your achievement! Women will faint in your path and you will revive them. They will build a triumphal way for you and hang wreaths of violets around your . . . monument. Your . . . image will be in the dreams of all our fair maidens and your manhood will be a site of pilgrimage where extraordinary conversions will take place. You will become a phallic symbol, the greatest honor that can befall a man! Go ahead, get laid, it's your turn!"

The poor bastard Party member has a moment of doubt.

But he is young, he is full of fire, he belongs to a master race, and he believes in his system. He yells *"Deutschland über alles!"* and rushes forward.

Tfou, tfou, tfou.

Florian winks at me.

"I give him three minutes, taking into account his strong constitution, his exceptional temperament, and the strength of his convictions. Nevertheless . . . what defeated Napoleon was the cold."

I am not listening to him. I pick a few flowers, violets, daisies, lilies-of-the-valley. I shall offer them to my beloved when she returns.

22.

De Gaulle Came Here

I was not aware that Florian had noticed my presence. And then I remember that here, in the Forest of Geist, and in a few other famous places, I cease to be a mere statistic and become perfectly visible. I grow suddenly to gigantic proportions. I can tell that at once from people's faces. You would think that I fill all the space, that they can see nothing else except me. I find this rather embarrassing. I was rather short when I was alive, and I made people laugh. I was often criticized for that: they said I lacked dignity. So, when I feel that I am growing to monumental, historical proportions in people's eyes, I am annoyed. I do not feel myself anymore. I have behind me far too long a habit of ridicule, I am too used to provoking laughter. There has always been something irresistible about my appearance, in my wild Harpo Marx hair, the ingratiating—some said lowly—smile on my lips. I do my best to appear tragic, noble, impressive: I put one foot forward and throw my head back, which is my idea of a heroic stance. I am afraid of disappointing people. It is a big responsibility, to be thus suddenly landed with greatness. When General de Gaulle came here on a pilgrimage with a lot of officials he stood to attention and greeted me with a military salute. I felt so embarrassed I almost got the giggles. It was nerves, of course, but go and explain that to Moshe Dayan and his new Jews. I had the impression that the eyes of all

Israel were upon me, and over there they don't treat a saluting general as a joke, which is the way I felt about it. I have to say this for myself: I managed not to laugh and not to come up with a wisecrack or a nice piece of my comical routine. I overcame centuries and centuries of Jewish stories, jokes, and caricature. It was very difficult and I had to make a big effort and tried to think of something sad. But what can still be sad, if you have had my experience? Nothing. Nothing is ever sad again. If you are the holder of a historical world record for sadness, all that is left for you to hang onto is your sense of humor. So I sprang to attention, lifted my eyes, and saluted. General de Gaulle was saluting me, and I, the Jewish dybbuk suddenly become visible and grown to heroic proportions, I was saluting him too.

But I'm telling you: it was terrible. There were at least fifty people there, they could all see me—I could read that in their eyes—a first-class audience, perhaps my last audience, and I could not allow myself to make them laugh. Heartbreaking. To recover, I had to sit up till dawn telling Schatzchen Jewish stories. He spent the night doubled up with laughter.

23.

Death Has a Flat

I draw nearer. I see a trace of sympathy in Florian's face. He is very fond of me. It was a job well done.

He takes a cigarette from his pocket and lights it. It goes out at once. He lights it again, but it's no use. The match itself goes out immediately in his fingers.

"Damn it!" he says dejectedly.

We all have our little problems, our little difficulties. It must be sad, never to be able to stroke a dog, tickle a cat's ear, or keep a bird or a living plant.

His shoulders and hat are covered with butterflies, lady-bugs, and cockroaches. The grass has withered all around him and no ants run near his feet. It is compulsive with him. He can't help it. He has no control over what he does. After all, Death too has to submit to his fate.

"Don't you sometimes feel you've had enough of it?"

He looks at me suspiciously. "Enough of what?"

I hesitate a little. I look at a swallow which has dropped at his feet.

"Of making love."

He is cross. He must see insinuations in everything.

"That's enough, Cohn. I appreciate Jewish humor very much, but I was with you at Auschwitz and so you've made me laugh again. I would also like to point out to you that

Beethoven was deaf, which did not prevent him from being the greatest musician in the world."

I lower my glance toward the heap of insects at his feet. "You aren't very choosy. You take anything."

He becomes morose. "There's a recession on at present. The market is saturated. People no longer want to pay. Orders are getting scarce. Even in Vietnam they only measure things with a dropper. Do you know what a great historical fresco costs? Millions. For Stalingrad alone they paid me three hundred thousand. The Jews coughed up six million. And besides, it takes time. In order to deliver *Guernica* I had to work for three years. And what did that bring me? A million and a half. That was bad business. A good epidemic brings me more. And yet, the Spanish Civil War is one of my masterpieces. It has everything—Spain, cruelty, Goya, light, passion, sacrifice. . . ."

I split my sides with laughter. In fact, if Death didn't exist, life would lose its comic aspect. Florian is flattered. He is rather vain. No one has ever been in greater need of an audience.

"Ever since Hitler and Stalin there has been inflation. Life wasn't worth much. I have had to raise my prices. For my last big job, the Second World War, I charged thirty million, and sometimes they seem to think that it wasn't too costly. I'm expecting a new order any minute now."

We both laugh. He's a natural, that Florian. At the Schwarze Shikse, we could have done a very funny act together.

"How are things going in Israel?" he asks softly.

"All right, thanks," I say, rather sharply.

"You know, if they want something really fine, I'll make them a special price. How many are they?"

"Two and a half million."

"For five hundred thousand, I'll make them a historical

fresco which will be the admiration of the world. How about it?"

"You've already done enough for the Jews."

"Look, three hundred thousand, because it's you."

I no longer want to laugh so much. The son of a bitch has really got History in his blood.

"You've become too expensive. I would like to remind you that to carry out your most beautiful work, two thousand years ago, you only needed one!"

"Yes, I know, it was dirt cheap. I was working for art's sake. But see what a lot it has brought me since then. From holy wars alone I've made millions. Come on, a hundred thousand, including the kids, and it's a deal. I'll do something unforgettable for you, something truly sublime. It will be worthy of Israel, I promise you. As it happens, I feel inspired."

"Look, there's a bluebottle. Go on, get your kicks."

He shrugs his shoulders.

I can't help stealing a glance in the direction of the horizon from time to time. I'm sentimental. I know that Lily is quite near us, in the bushes, doing her best, but with the dreamers of the ghetto it's an old habit: we always look for her in the direction of the blue yonder. I try to assume a casual air, but Florian caught the furtive glance I gave just then. I notice a slight, barely perceptible trace of irony in that ageless, unlined face.

"She's being laid by another superman."

If he thinks I'm jealous, he's mistaken.

"Besides, I thought that she'd already given you everything," he adds.

I pick a daisy and say nothing. I am not prepared to discuss my love life with an old pimp.

"She's very generous with herself," says Florian. "She sometimes gives herself without even taking the time to see

vehemence of which surrounds rather than inhabits me, spite and indignation which do not spare me but which, very much to the contrary, are aimed at me as well as at each blade of grass and at the whole of our Mona Lisa. There is here a shame, a feeling of vileness and guilt, which would make one think of God, if the latter could lack perfection to such a degree. Such a desire to escape from everything that is human is not even polite. I feel vexed. Who does he think he is, this fellow who is trying to get rid of me? What does he want—to be a man? He is not going to succeed: such an achievement is impossible. Besides, he completely lacks compassion, goodness, pity, and if Man is created without compassion, goodness, pity, he will be back on the same old dung-heap as before. I allow myself to point out to him the fact that a creation like that has already taken place and that is why there is neither world nor man, only a vague, confused dream of I don't know whom, in which a dim civilization of I don't know what drags along, as well as a salt shaker, a bicycle pump, six pairs of universal socks, and a nice clean *Encyclopædia Britannica*. One thing, in any case, is certain: I am not at home here, and although it is a permanent and natural obsession with the Jews and, moreover, entirely to their credit, I feel threatened. I don't even know whether I think or am thought of, whether I suffer or am suffered, whether I haunt or am haunted. In short, I feel myself to be *possessed*. Do you realize what that means, for a dybbuk?

The light itself has taken on a brutal, raw aspect around me, as though it were about to sweep everything away. I won't go so far as to state that there is a real conscience there, it's unthinkable, a thing like that, unless it's conceivable that God is slowly wearing out, that a weakness has overcome him and thus made him vulnerable and accessible to pity.

The Jewish fist is still there, but the sewer from which it emerges is perhaps not the one I thought it was. I am not suggesting anything, I respect the soul as much as I respect the whole of literature, I don't pretend that my subconscious is any different from the others, it's what it is, and indeed I am sure that by looking closely one would even find Germany there, *tfou, tfou, tfou.* All that I am saying is that I am twisting and turning inside the tortured subconscious of an intellectual who has got the Warsaw ghetto on his mind, not to mention the goat, the absolute, the twisted spout of the watering can, and the little postman still full of warm mail.

I wonder if Florian can see the Jewish fist. I don't think so. He must have had so many angry fists thrust at his nose that he must believe them to be part of it.

"Everyone accuses you of having allowed yourselves to be massacred without resisting," he says. "Public opinion is outraged, the very fact that they were able to destroy you so easily has provoked a renewal of anti-Semitism. Why didn't you defend yourselves? Force of habit? Or did you have doubts about the Germans until the last minute?"

"I promise you we'll do better next time."

We both laugh. He's a dream, that Florian. In fact, I wonder what the promoters of Oberammergau are waiting for to make a musical comedy out of the agony of the Warsaw ghetto.

Decidedly, I am beginning to find the fellow who harbors me rather attractive. As we say in Yiddish, it's no longer love, it's pure hate. He becomes more attractive to me because I no longer believe that he is one hundred percent Christian: there is a lack of resignation in him.

I am beginning to know him a bit better. His way of treating death seems to betray a secret attraction, which he doubtless tries to resist. As for our legendary princess, I know what he thinks of her. A whore, a nymphomaniac, frigid, trash. He must be in love with her himself.

I'm going to give him a bit of a teasing.

"On the whole," I say loud and clear, "Lily is not to blame. The lack of real love is not her fault, and it's normal that she should keep looking for happiness. The blame lies elsewhere, you must look for it much higher up. . . . Lily is innocent."

What happens next is extraordinary. The Forest of Geist starts to sing. It is a splendid song of joy, of beauty, of gratitude. The fellow is even more of a bloody fool than I thought. Clearly, an idealist.

"Listen!" says Florian, astonished. "Can you hear?"

"Perhaps she has achieved satisfaction," I say.

Things at once start to settle down. The Forest of Geist darkens. If that guy doesn't know me yet, he'll still get some surprises.

"I distinctly heard heavenly choirs," says Florian anxiously.

"I don't think it's what you believe it is," I say. "God wouldn't be interested in doing that for her. It's always spiritual with Him."

"I don't believe anything at all," confirms Florian with emphasis.

"I'm sure I've guessed your thoughts," I say severely.

"I didn't think anything of the kind," Florian retorts. "It's disgraceful. I cannot allow myself to have such thoughts. Blasphemy is strictly forbidden to me."

"It's disgusting," I say. "You ought to be ashamed of yourself. One can hear heavenly choirs without immediately imagining that up there it is the end of impotence and that God has decided to put an end to her frustration and——"

This time, he is completely panic-stricken. He changes

color. If you want to know what it's like for Death to be afraid, you only need to show disrespect to his master. He's a lackey, that Florian.

"I forbid you," he screams, in a eunuch's voice. "I forbid you to mix up God with what is happening here!"

"I didn't know you were so superstitious," I say, with the greatest sweetness.

He becomes completely paralyzed. Drops of sweat appear on his forehead, and the idea that a little dew can come out of that utter dryness warms my heart. He tries to speak, but only the stale smell of garlic sausage comes out of his mouth.

And it is at this moment that something even more satisfying occurs. Some pretty yellow butterflies approach Florian, fly around his head and . . . *nothing happens!* The butterflies continue to quiver under his nose.

"For God's sake!" shouts Florian. "I am impotent!"

I try to reassure him. "It's nothing, it's just nerves. You're not used to it. Pull yourself together."

He pulls himself together. He stares fixedly at the butterflies. But nothing happens, they continue to hover, sweetly.

"I am dishonored!" barks Florian.

"No, no, not at all. A little breakdown. It happens to the best of us. Overwork. Insomnia, all those nights you spend at sick peoples' bedsides. . . ."

I really believe that Florian is going to faint. A real wail of despair rises from his entrails.

"I have a breakdown! Me, a breakdown!"

I sniff at a daisy. "Don't strain yourself, Relax."

He gives me a murderous look. "I *am* relaxed."

"Think of something else. . . . Tell me, what happened to García Lorca?"

"What about García Lorca? If one no longer has the right

to execute a poet at dawn there won't be any poetry left! I . . . I'm not feeling well . . ."

"You're not going to die, I hope?"

But he has lost all his sense of humor. "Very funny," he mutters between his teeth.

"Try again. Look, there's a fly over there . . ." ·

He withers me with a glance. "What the hell do you expect me to do with a fly?"

"I don't know," I reply tactfully.

But he is so panic-stricken that he stops at nothing. "The fly will do. Where is it? I need to be reassured."

It's a little fly, all airy and blue, buzzing prettily around a poppy. Florian creeps stealthily up to it.

"She's not bad," he says.

The fly goes "buzz." Florian runs after it, the fly has already moved on elsewhere. Buzz, buzz, and super-buzz, a real little tease. She finally alights in the grass and Florian leans over her. There is a rather moving moment of silence. Poets call that the moment of truth.

"That's all right," says Florian. "I got her! Ouf!"

The fly at once buzzes away.

"Ts-ts," I say sympathetically. "Missed again."

Florian flings himself down on a rock. He is so hard hit that his face takes on some color. "It's not possible," he says hoarsely. "I've lost my powers! I can't manage it anymore! I can't even kill a fly! Me, the death of Caesar and of Robespierre!"

"People strongly recommend Royal Jelly," I tell him.

I believe he is going to choke.

"Ho, so you're being funny! You think anything's allowed! Just because I . . . draw a blank! Anyhow, who made Verdun? Who made Stalingrad? I have made war, I have!"

"Just one way of reassuring yourself about your virility," I tell him.

I feel better and better, where I am now. It is rare for a dybbuk to feel sympathy for the person whom he haunts, but this fellow, he's a brother. For once, I have hit on an authentic enemy of the established order, of the nature of things, of nature itself.

Not to mention his enormous *hutzpeh*. You've got to have monstrous cheek to dream of reducing death to impotence like that.

I wonder nevertheless whether I won't help Florian to get himself out of this trap. In any case, even if Death didn't exist, men would invent something even more revolting. Florian does limit their possibilities a bit, in spite of everything. And I think of Lily. One cannot leave her without a solution, without any hope. Eternity is all very fine, but I'm not at all sure that it's the way to reach a climax.

"Listen," I say to him. "There's a subversive dirty dog who is using intimidation to try and get rid of you, of me, of Lily, of the whole world . . ."

He is not listening to me. He is terrified. His eyes goggle, he looks completely half-witted. He prods himself.

"What's that?" he mutters. "I feel a suspicious beating, here, on the left. . . . It palpitates, it thumps . . ."

"The heart," I say, rather horrified myself.

"What?"

"You're growing a heart. . . ."

A thing like that, I wouldn't wish it on my best friend.

At first he doesn't understand.

"You poor bastard," I say to him. "Someone has played a really dirty trick on you. They've bloody well stuck a heart into you. I don't want to alarm you, but I think it's even more serious than that. *You've become alive!*"

148

He lets out a yell: I've never heard anything like it, and I've been well educated.

"Help!" he barks, in an already expiring voice.

A real birth.

"Do you want me to send for a doctor?"

"Certainly not. I know all about them. . . . To do that to *me!* I don't want to be alive. I'm too fond of life, I am!"

He jumps to his feet. "Alive! I'm alive! It's ghastly! I can't face it! Blindfold me, someone!"

Suddenly, I have the sensation of getting lost. The void overcomes me, a kind of indifference, somnolence, and if someone shouted "Germany" at me, I wouldn't even say *tfou, tfou, tfou.* Everything fades away, forgetfulness overcomes me, everything becomes distant, the page is turned, one mustn't think about such things anymore, it's over, the slate is wiped clean, I disappear from sight, I melt away, they wash me, they scrub me, they clean me, it smells good, it's clean, at last one will be able to forget. Nothing matters to me anymore, as though I were becoming a man, that classical way of giving up the ghost. The Jewish fist is still sticking out of the sewer, but now I am not even sure if it is not merely a work of art.

I am on the point of disappearing without a trace when my exterminated person's instinct for self-preservation gets the upper hand. I understand in a flash what is happening. It is a peril which never ceased to weigh on the minds of dybbuks, be they one or six million.

They are trying to exorcise me.

I put my hand on my yellow star. Ouf! It's still there. All my strength returns at once.

"What's the matter?" asks Florian. "You made an odd face."

He is sitting quietly in front of me, cleaning his nails with the point of his knife.

I say nothing. I hold my breath. Even if tradition were observed, even if ten Jews famous for their piety surrounded me and prayed according to all the rules of our holy Torah, I would still refuse to disappear.

If they really want to exorcise me, they've only got to do what they have never yet done: *create the world*. I'm not saying create a new world: I say, *create the world*. It will indeed be for the first time.

I wouldn't accept anything less.

And then . . . The ancient messianic dream is still in me. I think of Lily. She must be helped to fulfill herself. No man has the right to renounce this mission.

"Tell me . . ."

Florian looks up.

"Yes?"

"The Warsaw ghetto . . . She was there, wasn't she?"

"Surely. You have no idea of the kind of places she turns up in."

"She must at least have felt moved, didn't she?"

"Of course. Lily is easily moved. That is her whole tragedy."

"And . . . nothing?"

"Nothing. She remained moved, that's all. And now, if you'll excuse me . . ."

He looks at his watch and takes out his knife. "Three minutes. He must have already made a success of his life, that young man, over there."

He moves away. The fist is still there. I have always regretted not having been to the Warsaw ghetto, with the others. I used to know Nalewki Street well, before the war. It was a place full of little fellows like me, who all looked very much like caricatures: the anti-Semites had a real genius for caricatures. Even the names were comical: *Zigel-baum, Katzenelenbogen, Schwanz, Gedanke, Gesundheit, Gutgemacht.*

My place was in there, with all of them. It's strange there are Jews who will die with the feeling of having escaped death.

24.

The Elite Once More

Thus, I am about to give way to the temptation to be serious, which is terribly dangerous for a clown and which has already cost us the loss of Charlie Chaplin, when I hear an animated conversation going on quite close to me and I see the two distinguished aristocrats, Baron von Pritwitz and Count zu Zahn, emerge into a clearing. I must admit that, in spite of their long race through the holes, the mud, and the uneven ground of the Forest of Geist, the two men have kept their elegance, and their clothes are as impeccable as those worn in the age of Goethe. There are certain well-born souls who not only know how to dress but also how to preserve their immaculate appearance and their well-starched dignity against wind and tide. The Baron's suit of Prince-of-Wales check appears to have come straight from the hands of an eager valet, and it is certain that our elite, in spite of all the supposed difficulty of finding good servants, will never lack thinkers and aesthetes who are past masters in the art of taking good care that no speck of dust, no tear of reality, shall soil a wardrobe for whose upkeep they have been responsible for centuries. About thirty years ago an interesting French writer, one who later proved himself in this kind of valet employment under the Nazis, launched a slogan which has since been adopted by a great number of our tradesmen: *we want clean corpses.* It was the biggest cultural order of the century.

The Baron is, however, slightly out of breath. The journey has exhausted him. His mug is marked by boundless astonishment. He really seems to be at the end of his tether. His eyes have a wounded, shocked expression. Nor is the Count zu Zahn in very good shape; he looks like someone who has several million dead at his heels and as many others ahead of him. On his exhausted face only his white moustache preserves his dignity. He resembles a Don Quixote suddenly turning into a Sancho Panza. He is sweating profusely; he takes an ivory-white silk handkerchief out of his pocket and presses it to his forehead.

"And what can you do about it, my dear Baron? They will lynch her. They feel deeply humiliated, struck by her in their most sensitive place. . . . We are coming to the greatest crime of impotence of all time."

"Oh, my dear Count, democracy, what horror! Lily has fallen into the hands of the plebs. Those people are incapable of seeing her through the eyes of the spirit. They do not know how to love her as we have done throughout the centuries, with a purely spiritual love. The masses, giving way to the most primitive instincts—hunger, for instance: is there a more animal, more elementary instinct than hunger? —cannot manage to think otherwise than with their stomachs. What vileness, what bestiality! How can she possibly escape from them? Such an ancient, noble family! Such wonderful castles! Believe me, there is nothing left for noble souls but to know how to die!"

He notices the books lying on the ruins, and seizes them.

"Look, dear friend, look . . . books! It is she! She must be somewhere there . . . *Les grands cimetières sous la lune* . . . Montaigne, Pascal . . . *No Orchids for Miss Blandish* . . . *Le Musée Imaginaire* . . . Shakespeare . . . *La condition hu-*

153

maine . . . La reine des pommes . . . It is she, I tell you! *The impotent man . . . The frigid woman . . .* Quick; Lily cannot be far away!"

They charge off toward the horizon and disappear in the undergrowth. I hear little birds. I see butterflies. The flowers suddenly seem more beautiful, as always happens when there is nobody there. Nature recovers hope, holds up her head again, clearly starts to breathe once more. And to hope once more. I don't know whether you are aware of it, but Nature lives on hope. She hides very great expectations in her breast. Yes indeed, she too is rather a dreamer, she never loses courage. She means to make it one day. Or rather, to return to it. The return to Paradise, the Eden of her beginnings. She counts a great deal on man for that. On his disappearance, I mean.

25.

Shwarze Shikse

I give a jump. The butterflies vanish, the flowers wither, the birds drop dead in full song: Florian returns. He is leading Lily by the hand. Her clothes and her hair are somewhat disordered: the police have done their best. But I notice at once that yet again the police have not succeeded, any more than the army, the Church, science, or philosophy. On her features, which are of the purity of marble which no stains can ever mark, on this face which belongs to the madonna of the frescoes and the princess of the legends, there are tears, and tears are perhaps the only release which men will ever be able to offer her.

Florian has a little Dutch cigar between his teeth, which has never gone out. I don't know why I decide that that cigar is Dutch. Perhaps it's because Florian wears that expression of satisfaction which follows a well-settled business matter which one always associates with tidiness and the middle class.

"Well, one can say that our police are really expeditious!"

He stops, takes the cigar from his mouth, and eyes Lily with a piercing look. With his felt hat pushed back, that unbelievable bottle-green suit, his waistcoat draped with a gold watch chain and his patent leather side-buttoned shoes, he reeks of vulgarity and bad taste, which is rather surprising when you think that he is someone who has given us the works of Aeschylus, Shakespeare, and Goya, and who has always been the principal purveyor to our museums.

He pulls a handkerchief from his pocket.

"Careful, peach, you've got something on your eyelid. . . . A little impurity. Let me remove it. . . ."

Lily shuts her eyes and holds up her face to him. Light bathes her features. The perfection of this face is a real apotheosis of everything that the hand of man can ever accomplish, even in his most strenuous pursuits. I am overcome by a flood of warmth, a victory of my ineradicable love over the laws of nature. She never appears more moving than when she rises yet again intact from our ashes. I only have to go on keeping my eyes shut in order to see her in all her beauty. My beloved master, Rabbi Zur of Bialystok, always told me: "Moshe, it is not even enough to be blind, to see Humanity as one should. You've got to know how to *imagine* her too. It is a rare talent, Moshele, given only to the best of us. The others only know how to shut their eyes." Rabbi Zur was right. If nobody dreams about humanity, humanity will never be created. I keep my eyelids lowered and I look at her with all my heart. Her very long dress, on a corner of which I believe I recognize the signature of Piero della Francesca, has lost none of its splendor, in spite of some more obvious traces of the passage of man. It seems that even the most gifted cop, at work, in full possession of all his powers and doing his best, cannot tarnish her and deprive her of her beauty.

She remains thus for a moment, with her face thrust forward. Very delicately, Florian wipes her eyelid.

"A speck of dust. . . . There, it's gone. Nothing must spoil your perfection, luv."

"I'm always afraid of getting dirty," she says. "I have a horror of stains."

Florian stands back a little and admires her, cigar between

his teeth, thumbs in his waistcoat pockets. An expression of pride comes over his face. His voice sounds even more hollow, one feels that he is moved.

"Oh, I can promise you, it's a pleasure to look at you. I'm an old pimp, but you really are the most beautiful of them all."

She smiles at him, lays her hand on his arm. "You are nice. And besides, you—at least—you know how to love."

"Thank you, luv. It's because I've got what it takes, or, if you prefer, because I've not got what they have. They are full of . . . reality. They overflow with it. They are handicapped by their . . . ahem! by physiology, that's it. Physiology—and organs—are a real infirmity."

She hesitates for a moment. "Florian . . ."

"Yes, peach. Anything you want. You only have to say the word, and I'll kill the lot."

"Florian, and if I told you that I've never loved anyone but you? I've always known, deep down inside me, that you are the only one who can give me what I seek. But you won't have anything to do with me, there. You like to see me suffer."

This time, Florian's smile shows itself sufficiently and remains on his face long enough for me at last to recognize the fellow's profound nature: total and absolute cynicism, without beginning and without end, the smile of eternity itself which prowls around man.

"Put yourself in my place, my pet. If I were to take you completely, what would there be left for me? Little birds, and flowers? Pooh! I would end by gobbling myself up, out of frustration. . . . Come on, luv, don't be discouraged."

He raises his arm, a rather theatrical gesture, there's something of the barnstormer in that scoundrel. One feels that he has seen plenty of melodrama. He declaims:

"Listen to this earth which sings with the voices of a thou-

sand crickets of a hope which no human adventure will ever be able to deceive . . ."

It's better than I thought. Cervantes. The son of a bitch is a plagiarist, to boot!

Lily taps her foot in anger. "What do you expect me to do with a lot of stupid crickets?"

Florian is rather embarrassed. "Anyhow, you have just made another man happy, luv. It counts all the same."

That's a bit better. She likes to do good.

"You're the only one who understands me, Florian. I wonder whether true, great love isn't just that: two beings who never meet?"

"Yes, that can be very beautiful."

I myself feel quite moved. I had never realized that I must have lived through a very great love when I was alive: I never met the woman of my life.

I am meditating on my past happiness, when Lily lets out a cry. What I see is absolutely flabbergasting: Florian is crying. Yes, and for once it is not with the tears of other people.

"Florian, you're crying? You!"

"This dog's life!" wails Florian. "I get fed up with it sometimes."

"But what is it? What's the matter now?"

"What's the matter, what's the matter? . . . There are moments when I would like to . . . well, when I too would like to be able to . . . Watching them do it all the time . . . it's upsetting, in the end!"

"You would like to? You would like to be able to?"

"Well, nobody's perfect."

"Oh, Florian . . . You mustn't!"

"I'm not saying I want to be a man. No, not that, thanks awfully. But they end by getting on my nerves. . . ."

"You shouldn't envy them."

158

"All I can say is that it looks damned good. You've only got to look at their faces . . ."

"But they pass so quickly! A man, Florian, as you should know better than anyone, only passes. He retreats almost at once. It's so ephemeral! They always talk about building for a thousand years, but when they actually get down to the job . . . A thousand years! They make me laugh."

"Yes, I know, it's always that dream of endurance. It's a well-known symptom. They're all impotent."

Florian has completely regained his serenity, for the moment. "They talk about ecstasy, paradise, unheard-of happiness, and then they go glug-glug and fall over backwards."

"And they call that living! Well, luv, it's their little profit."

I have moved closer to Lily, in spite of myself. In my condition, I ought to keep quiet, that's what it's for, but not at all, it's stronger than I am. I am irresistibly attracted by her. It's hereditary with us, we dreamers of the ghetto. We are well known for our love of abstraction. Florian glances at me ironically.

"I should have suspected it. As soon as people start talking about profit . . ."

I laugh.

"That's just it, isn't it?" I say to him. "Of course, they ought to have built a Stock Exchange or a bank on the ruins of Auschwitz. That would have resuscitated us."

26.

Shwarze Shikse
(continued)

I go nearer. Lily pays no attention to me. She hasn't even smiled. And yet, what I have just said seems fairly funny to me. It's in the best humorous tradition of the Shwarze Shikse, which was incontestably the finest Yiddish cabaret and became world-famous after our first and greatest comic success, *Universal Love,* probably the best known *shtik* of the whole Jewish repertoire.

Florian seems amused. He shakes his finger at me in a friendly way.

"Mr. Cohn, you are beginning to irritate us, with your sores and your bruises. What do you expect? That we should bump off a hundred million Chinese just to prove that we aren't anti-Semitic?"

That's a good line, but no, Lily is not even listening to us. She has picked up a book, *Les grands cimetières sous la lune,* by a French writer, and she is absentmindedly leafing through the pages.

"She isn't interested in blue jokes," Florian confides in me. "She has very big things in mind."

I smile politely, but this seems to me a bit brash. Florian ought not to go in for smut in the presence of such a high-ranking person.

"However," he adds, "one really must laugh sometimes, to help pass the time. Eternity calls for some distractions, some parlor games, practical jokes, and leg-pulls. This is indeed how man was created."

I am no longer listening to him. I draw a little closer to her. Timidly. Humbly. I very much want her to notice me and at the same time I feel deliciously afraid. All that's needed is the cane, the bowler hat, the little toothbrush moustache, and the enormous shoes, to give me back my personality.

Florian notices my little game and takes on a bantering, frankly cynical tone. "Come on, Cohn, you might at least say hello to her—you never stop making eyes at her."

But what would be the good? She wouldn't even recognize me. She has no memory.

Lily is sulking. She has put down the book and her expression is gloomy. All around her the Forest of Geist is making efforts of unbelievable beauty, but she doesn't even notice. Life-size Dürers rise up in front of her, Italian primitives overpolish the landscape, *The Burial of Count Orgaz* passes back and forth before her eyes, Raphael makes his cherubs rustle around her. But no, nothing happens, she dreams of reality and will take nothing less. Art, that small change of the absolute, doesn't interest her.

"Lily, look who is here. Do you recognize him? Genghis Cohn. Your oldest customer. Your faithful and tender lover, always ready to serve. Say hello to him."

"Hello," she says, with complete indifference.

I have the impression of dying just a little more.

"Come on, Lily, stop brooding! Don't you remember our friend Cohn? After everything you did to him!"

"It was very nice," say I gallantly.

She brightens a little. Her eyes have that fixed expression, that way of looking through you without seeing you which

161

is typical of certain women seized by a craving for an impossible happiness and who keep looking for a Messiah.

"How beautiful he is! What a forehead! Look at that forehead, Florian. . . ."

This time, even Florian is shocked. "Oh no, you've already had him. You're surely not going to go for him again, in the state he's in now? Lily, honestly!"

"Look at his eyes, Florian!"

I turn around very quickly to see whether there isn't another suitor queuing up behind me, but no, it's really me whom she wants to screw for the second time. *Mazel tov.*

"Look at his eyes, Florian. . . . What depth! How sweet it would be to live in his eyes, Florian, to take refuge in them forever."

"For God's sake, that's enough! Aren't you ashamed of yourself? *I tell you you've already done him!*"

"Oh?"

"Yes, of course!"

"That's a pity. And what did it produce?"

"What d'you mean, what did it produce? Nothing. Soap. Listen, I'm shocked. And yet, I didn't think I was capable of it. . . . Really, Lily, you might at least remember! It's not asking much."

"Cohn," I say timidly, "Genghis Cohn. Always ready to oblige."

"Don't know him."

"Lily!"

She makes a little obstinate face. "How can you expect me to remember everybody?"

"It's only polite."

"Look here, Florian, really. You talk to me as though I were a nymphomaniac. If I don't remember them, it's because they made no impression on me. They did nothing for me, they didn't even lift a finger . . ."

"Lily, please!"

"They always get out of it with a pirouette."

"Oh no, really! There are some who gave you everything! The other one . . . remember . . . what was his name now? The one who loved you so . . . Don't you remember him? You only made one mouthful of him. A very great tenor. You really thought you had met your match . . ."

"Camus? Yes, I remember very well. I've read his books. But it's not with books——"

"That's quite enough! It wasn't him, anyway. Wait . . . a word of five letters . . . It begins with a J . . ."

I try to help him. "Jacob?"

"No, of course not Jacob, damn it, not Jacob, not at all. Good God, I only know that——"

"Jaffe? The one from Pogromska Street?"

"No, of course not . . . Oh yes, Jesus, Jesus of Nazareth, doesn't that name mean anything to you?"

"Most certainly it does. I must have read it somewhere."

"Read it, read it? But for goodness' sake, it was your biggest and your best piece of business!"

This time, I get cross. "That's enough! You're not always to accuse us Jews of trying to do business! Can you tell me what business He did? A business like that, I wouldn't wish on my best friend."

27.

She Has a Taste
for Masterpieces

For the first time since we have known each other I see that
Florian is deeply shocked. I understand him. He is very
proud of his *Crucifixion* and of all the admirable art which
has resulted from it. In fact, he must rather believe himself
to be responsible for all the marvels of the Renaissance. But
Lily still keeps that little obstinate look of indifference. She
doesn't remember it, so there.

"Lily, look here! It really seemed to have done something
for you: cathedrals, civilization, the most beautiful songs . . .
Remorse, sobs . . . Mortifications!"

I scold her a bit, too. "On candles alone, do you realize
what you must have spent?"

She's had enough. She taps her foot. "You can't expect a
woman to remember every man she has been in love with
in her life."

Florian goes white with rage. It's surprising to see him
getting his natural color back again. His voice becomes hollow, all his tough old pimp's deep, secret obscenity shows
itself once more. "I'm going to have it out with her," he
snarls.

"Perhaps I'd better go away," I say tactfully.

"That's right. Humanists always shut their eyes at the

critical moment, when she shows herself in her true light. Afterwards, they say: it's not her, it's the Nazis! It's not her, it's Stalin! It's never her, it's never her fault, to them. You're going to stay here and look at her, Cohn, there's nothing like a *voyeur* for looking things squarely in the face."

Florian is so furious, so overexcited, that a little icy wind detaches itself from him and makes me shiver.

"Lily, one can be a bit absentminded, a bit flighty, a bit moody, but when one crucifies someone and makes Him the foundation of a civilization of two thousand years of love and artistic treasures, one remembers it, for God's sake. You declare that you are always disappointed, you accuse them all—and rightly, rightly!—of coldness and mediocrity of feeling, but when there is one of them who really has a heart without limits and who gives you the Passion, the true one, something classic, and who has been the admiration of the world and has had an enormous following, you can't just not remember Him!"

She ponders, and her face lights up. "Oh, it's true, I remember it now. I loved that. It was very pretty. It was, in fact, even more beautiful when it had been retouched a bit by Michelangelo. But He was sweet."

"Sweet?" yells Florian.

"He had very beautiful eyes. Moreover, they became even more beautiful when they were lit up with suffering."

For a split second, I think that Florian is going to choke. His breathing becomes a whistle. His lackluster eyes suddenly acquire an expression of outraged dignity. I realize that the Valet fears the anger of his Master.

Lily's eyes are drowned in sweetness. "I love expressive faces," she murmurs in a rather hoarse, deeply sensuous, little girl's voice. "Suffering gives a wonderful expression, something indescribable. . . . He was very beautiful, on His cross. It was well worthwhile."

165

"I'm going to do something desperate!" exclaims Florian.

"You already have," I say to him. "And who left Him up there for two days, for the sake of the masterpiece: You."

"It's not true," he stammers. "I have to let nature take its course."

"A course like that one, I don't wish on my best friend."

Lily observes him now with scorn. "You are rather indifferent to Culture, Florian. If He had not suffered, what a loss it would have been for humanity! You don't know anything about aesthetics."

"Lily!"

I rush to her aid. "Listen, one is allowed to have artistic leanings, she is right. If you hadn't committed that murder, the two of you, two thousand years ago, what a dead loss it would have been for culture! Not one icon, do you realize that? No Byzantine art, no Renaissance, nothing. No goodness, brotherliness, no universal love. One shudders to think of what might have happened if she hadn't crucified Me. Barbarism."

Florian seems dumbfounded. "Enough, Cohn! Who do you think you are, now?"

Lily shakes her glistening hair—all the art of Florence, of Venice, of Cellini, seems to have graced it—with sincere and disarming astonishment.

"How could I have forgotten Him? I had stopped there, on the way, I had even gone out of my way to give some orders. . . ."

"It's true," I say. "She neglected nothing, I can assure you. Each nail had been planted in the work with a loving care for detail, each sore already foretold Giotto and Cimabue. The blood hardly flowed, those almost invisible springs which will later become majestic rivers. Each bone was disarticulated, one could already foresee the genius of Gothic art. The execution was perhaps a little lacking in fullness, one felt that sooner or later the work would have to be en-larged, given epic proportions. . . .They've had to wait for twenty centuries, but they've succeeded."

I have the impression that Florian is beginning to distrust me. He observes me with close attention. But if he thinks that I'm going to parade about in front of them with a crown of thorns on my head and with each nail in its place, he's crazy. If they saw me in that state, they would rush to put me back in my place. Such a place, I don't wish it on my best friend.

Florian hesitates a little. He runs his tongue over his dry lips. He is worried. First of all, he has no orders. Further, he is unable to admit that I might still be in love with Lily, if it really was me. He knows that in my place he would be terribly angry with her. Not so much because of what she did to me two thousand years ago, but because of everything else she has gone on doing ever since.

He turns toward Lily. She has a marvelous smile on her lips. She remembers, for once; there is no doubt about it. Again he looks at me; I assume a mysterious air.

Florian is now so worried that Lily's voice makes him jump.

"I was very moved, Florian. Well, I was almost moved. I felt something, for the first time. But all the same, some-thing was missing. . . ."

"What?" asks Florian nervously. "What was still missing?"

"I don't know. A little something."

She snaps her fingers. That's it, she has remembered.

"Oh yes, I know. *It was too quick.* It didn't last long enough. They did it too fast, psh . . . psh . . . and it was all over."

Florian's pinched, white nostrils emit whistles of indig-nation. He is so overexcited that the little cold draft that comes from him turns into an icy wind.

"Lily, I'm going to get really angry."

I try to calm him.

"You mustn't. She's perfectly right. I only stayed up there two days. A trifle."

"He was so beautiful."

She ponders for a moment. A malicious smile rises to her lips.

"Florian?"

"What now?"

A slight, capricious air, authoritarian nevertheless.

"I want another one."

I believe I glimpse a trace of terror in Florian's eyes.

"It was admirable, that Crucifixion, Florian. I want to see one again."

"Wh–wh–what?"

"I want another one like that."

Death opens his mouth in astonishment, a mouth so wide that I can almost see Alexander the Great.

"Lily, it's not possible! I . . . I must have heard wrong. I'm getting deaf in my old age."

"It's all those screaming mothers who ruined your hearing," I tell him, reassuringly. "It's a very bad thing, noise."

"Lily, aren't you ashamed of yourself?"

Her lips tremble. I feel that she is on the verge of tears. I know what there is left for me to do.

28.

The Blue Danube

Just imagine a golden legend, the most beautiful tapestry in the world, a princess weeping in sublime light, and you will understand what I felt, I, Cohn of Nalewki Street, an obscure and insignificant person, ludicrous and much laughed at, to whom an unhoped-for opportunity suddenly presents itself.

"I want another one like that! On a hill, in an olive grove, something pretty . . ."

I take a step forward. "I would be most happy if I could be of service to you." Florian is indignant. "Masochist! Degenerate! Cohn, get the hell out of here, she's had you enough!"

Lily looks at me attentively. I feel deliciously moved. I have a hunch that civilization is going to be enriched by a new contribution.

"I am at your disposal."

Florian gives me a glance of utter disgust. "It only thinks of getting laid!"

"Apparently, I've already had you," says Lily.

"You're telling me," says Florian under his breath. "It cost a million a go, not including the soap!"

She opens her arms to me. "But I would like to dance with you. I adore the waltz." Florian tries to intervene. "You've already made him waltz enough, as it is."

She draws near. "Yes, but I can teach him some new steps . . ."

"They're always the same ones," Florian yells. "Cohn, get out, while there's still time! You've got to be as masochistic as a chamber pot to try and satisfy her!"

She is reaching out toward me. Say what you like, she knows a customer when she sees one.

"Come, Mr.— Your name, again?"

"Cohn. Genghis Cohn, censored Yiddish comedian, at your service."

"Come, Mr. Cohn, it will be our most beautiful, our most thrilling waltz!"

Believe it or not, the princess of the legends takes me in her arms and, at the same moment, the violins start up in the pit, in the orchestra pit I mean, I stand on tiptoe, I take off . . .

"*The Blue Danube,* damn it!" Florian shouts. "You really can't get yourself screwed again to the sound of the oldest tune in the world!"

"Closer, closer," murmurs Lily. "Hold me tighter . . . Yes, like that . . ."

A strange sweetness, a marvelous headiness overcomes me.

"Ex . . . cuse me . . ."

I let go of her, I clutch my throat, I am beginning to suffocate . . .

"Imbecile!" shouts Florian. "Cuckold! Humanist-shit!"

"It's nothing," says Lily. "It's *The Blue Danube,* it's going to your head."

Not at all, it comes from her, it's her scent. I recognize it.

"*Gas,*" I mutter. "Excuse me, but Your Ladyship smells of *gas!*"

"Fool!" Florian hurls at me. "I told you so! New steps, you're telling me! They're always the same ones!"

I am dancing all alone, for the moment. It's no longer the

waltz. It's one of our very old dances. Lily starts to applaud.

"How pretty! What is it, that dance?"

"It's the *hora*," says Florian. "It came to them quite naturally, like with cats on hot bricks. A folk dance. The Cossacks taught it to them."

Lily claps her hands in time. "Bravo, bravo!"

I don't know what's the matter with me, but I can't stop. My eyes are popping out of my head, the violins are sawing madly, I see myself surrounded by an audience of Nazis in brown shirts, all beating time except one, who is grinning and pulling a Hasidic Jew by his gray beard, and the old Jew is also laughing in an engaging way, both of them turned toward posterity.

"Help! help! I can't stop!"

Abruptly, I feel a powerful hand seizing me and shaking me, I suddenly get the impression that the whole of Israel is there, down to the last *sabra,* and that a whole country is pushing me, with huge kicks in the ass, toward the past.

"Bravo, well done!" Florian flings at me. "Get the hell out of here, you and your folk dancing! We're fed up to the teeth with Jewish folklore!"

29.

The German Miracle

I find myself back in the bushes, my head is still going round and round, the ground gives way beneath me, I hang onto something, at last I regain my sight. I notice that I have both hands tightly gripped around Schatz's leg.

"Let go of me!" he yells. "Can't you see that I'm burdened enough as it is?"

I notice, in fact, that he has his problems. He is floundering in a heap, the exact nature of which at first escapes me, but in which I recognize a goat, a mother-in-law worth ten of them, and an *Encyclopædia Britannica* in twelve volumes, while at the same time Schatz tries to push away the little postman still full of warm mail. I would like to help him, but I myself am rather hampered, I receive a salt shaker in the eye, a bicycle pump is bothering me from behind, I discover that I am holding the Mona Lisa in my arms and that I am surrounded by every kind of object of worship, amongst which I detect a goat, three Buddhas, two Stalins, six pairs of nice clean Mao Tse-tungs, a ton of saints with fluorescent halos, a *Kama Sutra* with an illustration on the cover of Marx and Freud in the same bed, a toothpick, ten kilos of Khmer art, one de Gaulle, two pairs of Zen breeches, eighteen Oedipus complexes in good condition, Rude's *La Marseillaise,* ten cattle trucks full of democracy, three red perils, one quite new yellow peril, a best-period human-skin lampshade sold with a Vermeer, an ass full of pity by Hieronymus Bosch, a complete set of Saint Sulpice Christs, twenty pairs of boots full of Jewish suffering, a whole collection of hearts which bleed when you insert a coin, thirteen civilizations which can still be of use, a completely drunken *La liberté ou la mort,* a leper's kiss (as a matter of fact, that is how the leper got infected in the first place), fifty humanist operas, a swan song, a crocodile tear, ten million clichés, a bicyclist who never arrived anywhere, and the skullcap of my beloved master, Rabbi Zur of Bialystok, still full of ecumenism. It's a real dump, that chap's subconscious.

We try to extricate ourselves. But the ground gives way under us, it's soft, it's sentimental, it's tender, one can still build on it for another thousand years of exploitation and make-believe.

Schatz is completely nauseated. "It's revolting!" he shouts. "I told you before that we had fallen into the clutches of a sex maniac!"

I look closely at Schatz. He's right. I burst out laughing.

"I hadn't ever noticed that you looked like that before!"

Schatz gets furious. "I don't. It's that son of a bitch who makes me look like that."

I can't stop laughing. The thought that they've at last managed to incarnate the famous virility of the Master Race in the person of Schatz fills me with hope. I didn't think that the German miracle could reach such proportions.

"You ought to try again," I tell him. "Maybe you'll give her satisfaction. You've got just the right appearance now. Try again, *mein Fuehrer!* Anyway, the first time you retreated too quickly."

"Cohn, don't you realize! That guy is trying to kick us out!"

I think it over. I try to imagine what Rabbi Zur would have advised me to do, if he were still in his skullcap. People have always asserted that the Jews have a destructive side, that their humor itself is a kind of unarmed aggression. It's possible. We are a race of dreamers, which means that we have never ceased to await the creation of the world. Several Talmudic considerations then spring to mind. One, that the guy is perhaps the Messiah, who has come at last to liberate men from their subconscious and to guide them toward the light. Two, perhaps we are floundering in God's subconscious, all of us, and He is trying to free Himself from us in order to have peace. Three, someone is really trying to create the world, therefore beginning at the beginning, that is to say, by sweeping away all the rubbish which encumbers us. Four, that the fellow is simply a sickened idealist, who's had enough of the Jews, of the Germans, and of the very semen of the species.

I am thus trying to orientate myself in the midst of this situation, when an outburst of voices reaches me from the direction of the clearing and I wonder whether Lily is not in mortal peril, for it is clear that if a true Creation is taking place, humanity has everything to fear. I push aside the bushes, I observe what's happening. Florian and Lily are after each other. Aha! Perhaps it is, indeed, the beginning of the end. If someone succeeds in making Florian lose his head, he is quite capable of killing her in a fit of rage.

He is going for her like a polecat.

"That's enough now! Try the Americans for a change! They're still fresh! The kikes, we've had enough of them! But no, you cling to your old habits!"

I am surprised by this vulgarity. Lily herself is shrieking, she looks more like a fury than a princess of the legends. She is disfigured by hatred. It's really most odd: her hair, which was so fair, has turned black. It's probably psychosomatic, but all the same, I'm worried. Her features have

174

taken on a pronounced Greek character, if not Gypsy, or even worse: she is beginning to look like my cousin Sarah.

"You're jealous! You're only a raucous old crow who can't fly anymore!"

"You're only dirty water, in which desire flounders about!"

"An undertaker's mute, a flunky whose soul also accepts tips!"

"A cigarette butt on which the whole of History has trodden."

"They are angry with each other," Schatz mutters beside me. He is very perspicacious.

Lily leans toward Florian in such a spasm of hatred that all the most beautiful images of our literary heritage spring to mind: a panther ready to pounce, an unleashed fury, Rude's *La Marseillaise,* the Rape of the Sabines, Charlotte Corday, the eternal feminine, and that supreme realization of literature, eyes which flash like lightning.

"Look! I spit in your face!"

"She is displeased," Schatz notes.

"I much prefer that to one of your kisses," Florian retorts.

"He's trying to pick a quarrel," Schatz observes.

But he's mistaken. It's only a lovers' spat and the perfect couple, the most united in the world, as yet runs no risk of separation. They remain silent for a moment, then approach each other with such a rush of tenderness, of ardor and emotion, that it gives me the shivers: there will be some more lovely massacres, I'm telling you.

"Oh, my Florian, what are we doing?"

"Forgive me, luv. We are suffering a little from overwork. Have a minute's rest. Come and sit on this stone here. Get your breath back."

"Florian, was I badly made, badly created? Maybe my detractors are right? Maybe I really am a little frigid?"

175

He puts his arm around her shoulders with infinite solicitude.

"You frigid, luv? Who can have put such ideas into your head?"

"I've read a book. Apparently there are such women who never manage it."

"That's only because other women are satisfied with very little, peach. They are the ones, obviously, who always manage it. Don't be discouraged, luv. Go on searching. You must pursue your spiritual quest."

"I'm so afraid of being mistaken for a nymphomaniac!"

"Now, that's a horrid word, luv. I never want to hear it on your lips again."

"You've no idea the things men ask me to do, to get themselves in the mood."

"It's always like that, when genuine inspiration is missing. Tricks. Techniques. Systems. Ideologies. They completely lack love. Impotent people always fall back on vice, my peach."

"That's true. I sometimes even wonder whether what they ask me to do to them isn't a bit disgusting. The other day, in Vietnam, they——"

"Mind you, that's a question of feelings. If it's done without passion, without love, when the heart isn't in it, then it's disgusting. But when it's done through idealism, when someone truly loves you, well then, luv, nothing is disgusting. You can do all kinds of things. Remember: they killed millions for the love of Christ. Millions for the love of Germany, or of France. During the French Revolution, they loved you so much that they even had to invent a new way of cutting off heads. As long as there is passion for you in their hearts, no matter what horrors they perform, they are merely making love to you, peach. They are trying to make you come."

"You're sweet, Florian. So understanding."

176

"I've become more tolerant, that's all. You mustn't be frightened or surprised when they ask you to do . . . certain things. You must help their virility to manifest itself. Even with a nuclear warhead, it still takes a lot of love, peach. How they love you in Vietnam, right now! How hard they try to please you! Why d'you think they're out there, killing and dying? Because they want you to be happy, luv. They do what they know how to do. Cynics, people who believe in nothing, are incapable of passion, luv. It's only those who truly believe in you who can kill a million people without hesitation. Sooner or later, they'll give you total fulfillment, peach. Your lovers are working toward an orgasm the like of which the world has never known. You'll taste at last absolute fulfillment . . . the true absolute. Not just the small change they all keep offering you. . . ."

30.

The Little Absolute

I am so fascinated by Lily that I don't even notice that something is happening, over there at the far end of the clearing, where the Forest of Geist reaches its full breadth. Schatz catches hold of my arm, and at the same time that Florian makes that interesting observation about sex being the small change of the absolute, a worthy citizen of Licht appears among the trees, followed by a pimply young man carrying an armful of books. The young man appears to be in a trance: he walks with his eyes raised toward the treetops, with a strange expression on his face.

"Oh, Papa . . ."

"Look down! I forbid you to look at that! By all means breathe in the air of the woods, the doctor says it will do you good, but keep your eyes on the ground! You are too young for that sort of thing! You must finish your studies first. Then you can marry a nice, decent girl."

The youngster suddenly stops and stares fixedly at a point in space with a smile which, in the light of my experience, I can only describe as dirty. The father is shocked.

"Wretched boy!"

"I can't help it, one of them is beckoning to me. Oh, and that one there! Look at it! How big, how beautiful it is! Oh, it's opening up, it's smiling at me!"

"What? It's smiling at you? Those things don't smile, you fool. Where? Show me! There's nothing there. You're going through an attack of puberty, that's all!"

"They're all over the place, on all the branches, with fuzz of every color, pale, dark, and red. . . . Oh, there's one that's all golden and curly. . . . Oh . . . Oh . . . And that one, look at that one, Papa! Can't you see? It's opened up wide and it's winking at me!"

I myself try to see, and I notice that Schatz too is craning his neck. This, no doubt, is not the real thing, the true, the great absolute, but what the hell, the little absolute is not to be despised either. It's always good to take. It relieves one.

"First of all, it was me it winked at, and further . . . there are no eyes in there! You don't even know what it looks like! It's an optical illusion! You've been working too hard at your metaphysics!"

"What pretty eyelashes they all have! How long and silky and trembling they are! Look, Papa, do look! There's a whole crowd of them!"

"I call this soliciting!"

"Oh . . . Some of them are winking and singing and cooing . . ."

"Cooing?"

"Oh, how they quiver, how they flutter about. . . . How they hover, and how they rustle! I love the red one! It must be so nice to——"

"Lower your eyes immediately! Aren't you ashamed of yourself! If your poor mother could only see you! The red one, do you say? Where is the red one? I can't see any red one."

"Yes, there, next to the Negro one . . . The one that's going chirp-chirp-chirp . . ."

"Chirp-chirp-chirp? They never do that. Those are birds,

you fool. It's their little fuzzy nests that you can see. I admit that their shapes are rather strange, but that's all."

"Ah, and that one there, which is going miaow, miaow!"

"It's a catbird. And on the public highway, too! I shall make a complaint. We aren't protected. . . . No, really, just look at that one! It's pure exhibitionism!"

"You're wrong to think of it all the time, Papa. Schopenhauer said that the taste for the absolute kills."

"You dare say that to me? I'll give you Schopenhauer! I've at least got eyes in my head, do you think you can hide your smut from me? Here, take that! Disgusting! In front of your own father! Go on, get out, back home with you!"

They go away. I shake my head. Dreaming humanity! Always that thirst for infinite joy!

"Genuine visionaries," says Florian. "You see, peach, you're not the only one to dream of the absolute. Limitless, spiritual needs devour the human soul. . . . Anyway, I've always had a weakness for redheads."

"The little fellow was sweet."

"He'll come back, peach. He'll be just ripe for the next war."

"Florian?"

"Yes, luv?"

"I've been thinking a lot about God lately."

"All right, luv. I'll bring Him to you as soon as He turns up."

31.

The Terrestrial Cow
and
the Celestial Bull

I am meditating thus on the unfathomable depths of the human soul, that ocean so rich in submerged treasures which sometimes reveal their exciting presence by such spiritual eddies on the surface, when I feel a hand on my shoulder. It's Schatz.

"I want to show you something."

I discover that Schatz, completely panic-stricken by the subversive elements that are prowling around us, has put on his military helmet, no doubt afraid of some new breaking loose of the heavens over his head. I notice at once that the helmet doesn't help matters; on the contrary. You must not think for a moment that I feel any unsurmountable hostility toward the proverbial German virility, but when it begins to assume such proportions I really have the right to feel indignant. I know quite well that Schatz has nothing to do with it, and that the cause of it is that positively unspeakable, degenerate subconscious into which we have fallen and which keeps playing its shameful tricks on us: the fact nevertheless remains that Schatz has no business exhibiting himself in a state like that. Neither am I ignorant of the fact that in the story by Gogol, "The Nose," the attribute in question had parted from its legitimate owner in order to saunter about the streets of St. Petersburg dressed in a brilliant red uniform; but for one thing, we are not in tsarist Russia, we are in the Forest of Geist, a lofty place where the spirit dwells, and for another, I would prefer to deal with any nose rather than with Schatz in his present aspect, *tfou, tfou, tfou!* I start hollering.

"You mustn't show yourself in such a state!"

"What's wrong with me?"

"Listen, Schatz, if you don't know what's happened to you, you've only got to feel yourself! You've no right to look like that, it's disgusting! You ought to go see a psychiatrist!"

Schatz goes green with rage, and I swear to you on the skullcap of my good master Rabbi Zur of Bialystok that it is one of the most frightful things that I have ever seen in my life. For a moment I cling to the hope that it's nothing, that perhaps it's Picasso, but the evidence is so realistic and so vivid that I cover my face! It's green, completely green!

A color like that, I wouldn't wish it on my best friend!

"So it's me who ought to be running to a psychiatrist?" Schatz bellows. "But it's you, Cohn, who see me this way! It's all in your head! You're a typical example of degenerate Jewish art, I've always said so!"

I open my eyes and force myself to look. As he has a helmet on his head, I have to examine him more closely, which merely ends in nauseating me. But at least it allows me to express my opinion.

"It's not *Jewish* art, I can assure you," I say firmly.

"All right, let's have it out," yells Schatz. "I didn't want to tell you, out of tact, and besides, I knew quite well that we were caught up in a subversive trap, both of us. I wasn't going to give in to that terrorist. But you ought to see yourself,

Cohn. You really ought to look at yourself, that's all I can say! Ha-ha-ha!"

I am horror-struck. I am about to put my hand up to my face, to feel it, but no, I'm not going to let myself be influenced by an alcoholic brute in full decay, a green decay, into the bargain.

"You're having hallucinations," I say to him with great dignity.

"Hallucinations? Cohn, feel yourself, see if you're a man! I will even add this, and I hope it will give you pleasure, for a man, you're some man, a real one, a hundred percent one from head to foot, there's no doubt about that, ha-ha-ha!"

I draw myself up proudly. I assume a slightly nonchalant air. I wiggle my ears a bit, to reassure myself, but this perfectly inoffensive movement has the effect of plunging Schatz into irrepressible hilarity. He is bent double with laughter, *tfou, tfou, tfou!* Absolutely terrifying to see, he points a finger at my face and shakes in uncontrollable giggles.

I go scarlet with fury and indignation. Now all of a sudden Schatz stops laughing. He seems frightened: he very quickly puts his hand over his eyes.

I am convinced. I no longer have any doubt about the hateful and terroristic treatment of which I am the object. And I know what it is.

"Cohn, I swear to you that this is not the moment for us to quarrel. We're both in the same shit. And that's not the end of it. Come here, I'll show you something."

I cannot imagine what on earth he can still have to show me.

"Thanks, I've seen enough."

"Come on, I tell you. Something terrible is brewing."

He says it with such conviction that I follow him in spite of myself.

As everyone knows, the Forest of Geist is a very elevated place, situated on the heights of the Licht mountains. Upon coming out of the woods, you have a very pretty view of the plain and the fields, with the smoke of Dachau on the horizon. I am relieved to see that the landscape has not altered. That guy certainly didn't spare our species, but perhaps just because of this he seems to have a certain consideration for nature. The fields and meadows have not been spoiled by any doubtful psychic elements. The air is pure and the sun is shining, the river sparkles gaily, everything is clean and tidy.

The only slightly disturbing element is this religious activity in the fields. I realize that I said "religious" instinctively, without thinking, perhaps because I have always been rather inclined toward mysticism, as you may have noticed, but in fact the nature of this pastoral activity is difficult to define precisely. It is possible that the white robes of many Dominicans mixing with the crowd may have influenced me. In any case, there is a considerable crowd there, in the meadows, enough to make one think that the whole population of the region has taken to the fields. From the heights where we are standing, it rather reminds one of a Brueghel, but the feverish activity in which all these good people are engaged is not like any familiar scene.

At first sight one might think that they are trying to toll a bell, but a bell which is not there. For this great human mass is harnessed to a rope which it is pulling with all its strength, and here is where I understand Schatz's anxiety. The rope, quite simply, disappears into the sky above.

I raise my nose in the air, I place a hand above my eyes, I scrutinize the sky with a piercing gaze, but the other end of the rope is not visible. It just vanishes into the blue yonder. So then, to what, to whom, to whose neck, can the rope possibly be attached? All these people seem to be pulling hard, as though meeting with some resistance. If it were a question simply of describing the action, I would say it was some peasants dragging a cow or a reluctant bull into a field. But it's not that. I really am unable to understand their intention, what they are trying to do. They are tugging this way and that, and yet the other end of the rope completely disappears into the void of the sky.

I try to summon the ghost of my good master Rabbi Zur to my help, but the *Cabala* itself, to my knowledge, contains nothing which could enlighten me.

And they sing. They tug on the rope like bargemen and they sing, and I believe I recognize the song of the Volga boatmen. A boat? I cannot see any trace of one, and anyhow, since when do boats navigate in the sky?

This is when Schatz formulates a hypothesis. It may not be worth much, but I would still rather have a hypothesis than nothing at all.

"It's for Lily," he says.

"What do you mean, for Lily?"

"They're fed up with her. She has exhausted them with her whims."

"So, what then?"

"They are sending for reinforcements."

"Reinforcements?"

"Listen, they have at last understood that only God can give her what she wants, so they are trying to bring Him down here, to give her satisfaction at last."

Humh. I feel rather vexed. I should have thought of it myself.

"You see, prayers, supplications, candles, all those have never been any good, so they are trying to bring God down here on earth."

The more I think of it, the more plausible this theological

hypothesis seems to me. The deeper you plunge into the sub-conscious, the more certain you are to find God in there. The only thing is to excavate. They're all the same, those cynics, romantic dreams hidden under the refuse. Ruins of the sky of admirable beauty. Absolutely intact prehistoric temples which only ask to be of use. Besides, I suppose that it works both ways. The more you plunge into a man's subconscious, the more certain you are of finding God, and the more you plunge into God's subconscious the surer you are of finding man, *tfou, tfou, tfou*.

I am struck by a delicate theological point.

"But, do you think they will like each other? In a case like that one cannot force anyone's hand . . . or whatever. There must be a minimum of mutual attraction. Supposing they were completely revolted by each other? You couldn't possibly force them. It's not as though you were having a cow covered in a field."

"I know nothing about theology," says Schatz dejectedly. "All I know is that if somebody doesn't satisfy her soon, it will be the end."

Looking at it from another point of view, it is inconceivable that God should refuse to answer humanity's yearning and to fulfill its needs, once they are at last brought into each other's presence, in a nice green field, under favorable conditions. In fact, up to the present, He must have been embarrassed by the Church. It is clear that the Church doesn't have the right atmosphere. On the contrary, it has surrounded God with such an atmosphere of prudishness, and it has such a holy horror of the body and of physical pleasure, that even with the best will in the world the noblest nature would hesitate to perform. The Church must have completely inhibited God. I speak only of our ancient Judeo-Christian church, for in the Bodhisattva an accomplishment such as this is expressly foreseen and awaited. It is possible—I can only formulate a hypothesis because, my good master of Bialystok no longer being there, I cannot benefit from his spiritual help—I say therefore that it is possible that our church, through this abstract, etiolated, prudish, disincarnate atmosphere which it has created around God and His virtue, through the constant stern supervision with which it has surrounded Him, has succeeded in giving Him complexes and, if not rendering Him impotent, at least in intimidating Him. Perhaps our ancient Judeo-Christian church has also succeeded in converting God Himself, and in making him feel disgust for the body and its needs. One understands then why if it is a question of providing for the earthly, physical happiness of humanity, and not just its posthumous happiness, God should have ended by having scruples and finding serious difficulties, that He should have become the prisoner of our prejudices and our cult of pain, and that He should thus have become completely inhibited, not daring to manifest Himself in all His power. Meanwhile, Lily suffers in all her poor body.

"Perhaps she ought to be warned," I say to Schatz. "It's a very big thing, a thing like that. It mustn't come as a shock. There is a risk of traumatizing her for good."

Schatz is becoming more and more depressed. "And suppose she doesn't inspire Him?" he murmurs. "He hasn't really ever seen her from that angle. It was always a question of her soul before, not of her physical side. Suppose He takes one look at her and runs away?"

Think as I may, I can find nothing in the *Cabala* which enables me to solve this new theological problem.

"In any case, even with a rope around His neck it's not at all certain that He will allow Himself to be convinced," say I. "Perhaps it would be better to avoid raising Lily's hopes. Let things follow their own course and——"

I am interrupted by a very distant sound, which I know well and which I have never known how to resist. I turn my back on Schatz and return very quickly into the Forest of Geist.

32.

A Sound of Hunting

A deep and virile sound is coming from the depths of the woods. I believe that I am the only one to hear it: we have particularly sharp hearing, our whole history is one long exercise in listening. With our ears glued to the ghetto wall we waited in vain for the slightest echo of the approach of rescuers, of outside help. Nobody ever came, but through straining our ears, our hearing became very acute and we became a people of musicians. Horowitz, Rubinstein, Menuhin, Heifetz, Gershwin, and a thousand others owe everything to our ancestors waiting and listening in our villages, lost in the Russian plains. With our ears always pricked, we learned to discern the gallop of Cossack horses before they reached us with their swords drawn, and the tramp of boots in the streets of Amsterdam, or of the Ukrainian atamans of Holy Russia. Thus it is that, since the Diaspora, our ears have developed and acquired characteristics which they never had before: you have all noticed on the corpses of Jewish teen-agers of the ghetto—there are some very colorful films on the subject— very well-developed ears which Streicher and Goebbels regarded as typical of the Jewish race.

There is therefore nothing surprising in the fact that, for the moment, I seem to be the only one to hear the distant sound of the horn. It is very beautiful, because it comes from the far blue yonder. Then it comes nearer and this time Lily hears it, and Florian too. Even Schatz, who is not a bit given to nostalgia and who had just joined me in the bushes, shows some interest. I notice a dreamy look on Lily's face. She seems favorably impressed. The sound comes ever nearer, persists, rises, grows, with a kind of promising virility. Florian appears irritated.

"Don't listen, peach. He's showing off."

"I love the sound of the horn in the evening, in the darkening woods," Lily murmurs.

"All it means, luv, is that the hunt is on."

I wonder what on earth they can still be hunting.

The horn insists. Rather ponderously, I feel. It is coming from too near, now, it is too noticeable. It's there, and it makes us feel it. I make a wry face. But Schatz is interested: perhaps it's not the Fuehrer yet, but it's already von Thadden. As Mr. Galinsky, president of the Jewish community of Berlin, has pointed out, there are already promising headlines on the front page: GERMANY CORRUPTED BY JEWISH PRESS.

The horn is now so near that Lily begins to tremble.

"He plays it so well," she murmurs. "I do love the horn, Florian."

"We've already tried music, peach. It didn't solve our problems. The true, great instrument doesn't exist. Men are working on it, of course. There's hope, a true love may soon come and grace us all: indeed, peach, our scientists are working on an artificial heart."

"It's coming nearer," Lily whispers.

I feel that she is on the verge of swooning. It is an unforgettable picture: the Forest, the flowers, the sound of the horn, it's all there. That is how our princess of the legends appears on all our priceless tapestries.

"Be careful," says Florian. "When one hears the sound of the horn in the midst of the woods, it's always very beautiful, very promising, but in the end all it means is that there are fierce dogs around."

The huntsman comes out of the thicket. He still holds the horn to his lips. He sees Lily and he takes a flattering pose. He is wearing *Lederhosen* and a small Tyrolean hat. He's a very handsome man, well proportioned, with plenty of beef just where it ought to be, his eyes are velvety, and of a rare stupidity. It's what we call in Yiddish a real ass-face. A fine moustache. He doesn't look German. He could have come out of a Maupassant story, with his stallion expression, or out of an impressionist picture full of beautiful males, with oars, in rowing jerseys, with long moustaches. Lily smiles at him, and the huntsman adopts an even more alluring posture. He puts one foot forward, puffs out his cheeks, and, the horn proudly raised to the sky, gets ready to blow.

"Pig," exclaims Florian, with obvious irritation.

"What a beautiful instrument!" says Lily, with a trace of emotion in her voice.

He is flattered. "Thank you, madam."

"Thank you for what?" growls Florian. "Just you wait!"

He's not bothering anymore. The huntsman, who is plainly very well set up, is violently unattractive to him. I wonder whether Florian isn't just a bit jealous.

"A real blockhead," he says, without even lowering his voice.

The superman has not heard him. He has eyes only for Lily. I even get the impression that the horn has suddenly become paler in color in his hands. White hot. It's always the same. It suffices for her to cast a glance at them and each one believes himself to be the man of destiny. In fact, supermen do exist, and Nietzsche did not dream in vain. There was at least one of them who kept his promises. You must all have read about him in newspaper reports from Cuba, at the time of the dictator Batista. It wasn't the dictator, but another man, a real one, not a fraud. He was called Julio-the-Superman, and you could see him in those dives which in Batista's days were open to all, where you could go to contemplate superhuman perspectives. The phenomenon was truly prodigious. Seventeen women were brought to him, and with each one he reached the absolute. To prove fully to the public that he was a genuine superman, and wasn't cheating, he retreated each time at the supreme moment, so that the skeptics and the cynics, all those born detractors who do not believe in the power of man, could ascertain that he was not cheating and that he had really tasted perfection seventeen times. If Napoleon or Hitler had seen that, they would have sunk into black depression and would have developed an inferiority complex.

True greatness, that's what it is, when all's said and done.

Lily's face, that brilliance in her eyes, that sudden light that makes her even more beautiful, as she contemplates the huntsman's admirable and proud instrument, are something that I shall never forget for as long as I am dead. She steps forward among the daisies, and at the same instant, like a sign of some celestial benevolence in the Forest of Geist, twenty-seven Socrateses, seven Homers, fourteen Platos, twenty-seven Leibnizes, seventy-two Johann Sebastian Bachs, two little Handels, and three thousand four hundred Greek gods and Hindu divinities appear among the unicorns, together with other mythological beasts guarded by their natural shepherds, philosophers, museum curators, and poets, at the same time that a thousand vultures take flight, each one with a message of love and hope in its beak. What a tapestry, what a masterpiece, what genius, what magic! It is as though each blade of grass had begun to believe in a Messiah again.

"What a beautiful instrument! May I touch it?"

The huntsman is very surprised. He hadn't expected so much. He thinks it over ponderously.

"But . . . of course! I am very honored!"

"Honored, honored!" growls Florian. "You just wait!"

Lily touches the horn. "What perfect lines!"

"You flatter me, madam."

"Please play it."

The huntsman blows his horn. Now that the sound is so close, I find it hideous. Reality. It no longer has anything to do with distance, nostalgia, with the blue yonder. It is there, brutally, heavily. Reality is killing the dream. I discover that the sound of the horn is like the bellowing of bullocks on their way to the slaughterhouse, a sort of profound stupidity, and that it is really absolutely revolting. A sort of moo-oo-ooing of butcher's meat. The beautiful promise becomes a mere phraseology. But it affects Lily, that at least is certain.

"It's as though heaven itself is at last going to answer," she murmurs.

True enough: I can hear dogs barking in the distance.

"It is answering," Florian remarks.

Lily touches the horn, shyly at first, with that admirable hand which Leonardo drew, and then she begins to caress it.

"I love everything which rises toward the infinite, everything which points the way to heaven. . . ."

The huntsman bows gratefully. "I won the first prize in the horned-cattle competition at St. Wenceslas . . . Gold medal, madam."

She takes his arm. "Gold medal?"

"Yes, indeed, madam."

"Look at that brow, Florian! How high it is! What space! It could be a wall dedicated to the genius of a Giotto, of a Piero della Francesca!"

"Thank you, madam."

"Tss," says Florian. "It's always the same old wall and the same old trophy."

The princess of the legends brushes the brow with her fingers.

"The mark of destiny . . . He is an empire-builder. . . . Can't you hear the silence all around us? The world is holding its breath. Something extraordinary is going to happen. . . . Farewell, Florian. I shall no longer need your services. When I come back, you will not recognize me. I shall be someone else. Transformed, appeased, happy, gratified at last. You will be dismissed. You will no longer be allowed to cast your cynical shadow over the earth. I shall rise up high, very high, and I shall never come down again. . . ."

"Put a rug on the ground, luv, it's beginning to get quite chilly."

Lily lovingly squeezes the huntsman's arm and looks at him with a languorous eye in which a Jewish star twinkles.

"A gold medal!"

They move away. Almost at once I hear the sound of the horn: the huntsman is at work. It's very beautiful, very masculine, it vibrates, but it is rather brief.

A moment of silence, and then the sound of the horn rings out once again: it is noble, but it trembles slightly, one notices the effort. Genuine inspiration is not there. Talent, certainly, and possibilities, but not the sublime genius which could give Lily a reality equal to her longing. I wait. This time, the silence is much longer. The genius is somewhat out of breath. His tongue must be hanging out, he must be sweating great drops, waiting in vain for help from the sky. I make a face. Humh. Incontestable natural gifts, but they don't go very far. We've had all that before. Apparently if you read Mao Tse-tung your powers increase and you become the world's ping-pong champion, but it would surprise me if even seven hundred million Chinese could manage to make her reach it. She needs the Messiah. The real one. Endowed with real power. He'll come, I'm telling you. We must be patient. The Messiah will come. He will present Himself, He will take her by the hand and will give her at last what she has been awaiting for so long. It will be the end of the search, of frustration, of longing. It's even possible that there will be some survivors, one mustn't be pessimistic.

And then the sound of the horn rings out for the third time. It makes a very fine debut, it rises, it vibrates, it bellows, perhaps it's a bit nervous, a bit jerky, one might almost say a trifle deliberate, but at any rate, it lasts, it does its best . . . the strength of despair. Alas! the sound dies away, flounders, hiccups, is strangled, and ends abruptly in a kind of gurgle. Florian shakes his head and gets out his knife. That's the way it is.

"There you are. No one can achieve the impossible, as Mao Tse-tung himself will have to admit in the end."

33.

The Goat
and
the Mona Lisa

The huntsman goes away and I feel a little sad at the thought that hope will never be more than the sound of a horn in the woods, and I try to let my thoughts rise toward Him whom Rabbi Zur pointed out to me with so much love, with an accusing finger, and I wonder whether I ought not to do something positive and go and help the others pull the rope, instead of bewailing Lily's fate, when I perceive Baron von Pritwitz and Count zu Zahn emerging from the thicket. At the same time I realize that events are speeding up, that is to say, things are deteriorating, and that the terrorist who surrounds us on all sides has firmly decided to expel us, to vomit us from his subconscious, our noble claims and our petty needs, so that he can at last read his newspaper in peace. High-minded people in particular seem to arouse his spite and his hostility. Baron von Pritwitz, for instance—and yet, he did strictly nothing under the Nazis. nothing, absolutely nothing—is in a sorry state. He still carries his Stradivarius, but his clothes are covered with blood, which wouldn't matter at all, if his bow tie were not undone. To add to the horror, he is running around in circles, which is fairly understandable, as he is caught in the smile of a Hasidic Jew of seventy years, who is being dragged along by his beard by a German soldier, who also has a huge grin all over his face, in the company of other soldiers who surround the Baron and his Stradivarius with their smiles, all posing for the camera which the Mona Lisa holds in her hands.

"I had nothing to do with it!" yells the Baron, while trying to free himself from that Jewish smile which is soiling his clothes. "I sat it out quietly in my castle."

I notice that the Baron's arms are now laden with Stradivariuses, I can count at least twenty of them, and the Count, although he has lost his pants and is defending himself against a particularly ill-intentioned black goat and a salt shaker, has succeeded nevertheless in keeping in his hands a Culture in excellent condition, complete in six volumes, with inventories, covers, and portfolios, and he is looking at the Jewish fist rising from a sewer under his nose without a shudder.

"It's ghastly!" the Baron whispers in an expiring voice, in which the trace of a Bach fugue still lingers. *"They* are coming back!"

"We must do something!" cries the Count.

"Yes, but what?"

"We must do something final!"

The Count casts a wary glance around him. "We can't do that again!" he mutters. "It's still too soon, and anyhow there aren't enough of them left."

"My God," moans the Baron, "but really, the Arabs— what are they waiting for?"

His face suddenly brightens with a last glimmer of hope. He has an idea. It always starts like that.

"At all costs. we must make peace with them! Dear friend, that portrait . . ."

The Count is defending himself against the billy goat and the salt shaker, but he has not let go of his Culture. One cannot but admire him. The goat, in fact, abruptly changes its mind and starts to attack the Mona Lisa, who lifts up her skirt at once.

"What portrait?"

"The portrait of the Jew Max Jacob whom the Nazis exterminated, painted by the Jew Modigliani, who died all by himself, he was in such a hurry to escape what was coming! It will be enough to buy it from them, so that they will at least know that Germany is not shrinking from anything and that we are ready to forget! Quick, dear friend, let's run! There's still room in our museums!"

They try to disentangle themselves, the Count tries to recover the Mona Lisa, the goat is enraged, it was almost a moment of truth, the Baron lands a blow on its skull with his Stradivarius, Culture defends itself, I don't know which is the stinking goat and which is Culture in all this, and "all this" is bathed in the smile of the old Hasidic Jew who is being dragged along by the beard by a goat under the eyes of other goats who are all grinning and posing for Culture and posterity.

I suddenly have the feeling that I am *repeating* myself. I don't know whether you can see exactly all the implications of *repeating* oneself. In any case, if my Jewish *shtik* doesn't amuse you, go next door, to a competitor: there's no shortage of Negro joints and Vietnamese restaurants.

I watch the two aristocrats, who have at last succeeded in disengaging themselves and are disappearing into the Forest of Geist. I can understand the dismay which overtakes high-minded people when spiritual values completely collapse on the Stock Exchange. But they are wrong. It is at the time of a slump, when cultural blue chips are at their lowest, that one should buy. It is true that not one among us, at Auschwitz, foresaw the German miracle. One could have gambled on it and made a profitable investment. Hitler offered us the opportunity to make a killing, and we ignored it. We're not as clever as people make out.

The Jewish fist is still there. I am beginning to wonder whether he isn't also aiming at me, whether that fellow isn't even more rabid than I thought. But not at all. It must be merely a monument. I decide to go and look at it close up, when I notice Lily and Florian coming back. Lily doesn't seem as indifferent as before, on the contrary, she looks even more desperate. Well, at any rate, it's better than nothing, at least she has felt something. Florian holds the horn in his hand, he collects trophies, the beast.

"We must hurry, luv. The train leaves in half an hour, Dr. Klaps is waiting for us, don't forget. What a miraculous man! Do you remember the society woman who always insisted that someone should knock on the door, while . . . seven short knocks, one long? And the one who could only surrender to happiness in the Subway, during the rush hour? And the one who could only rise to heaven in an elevator, and the one who had to have a revolver pressed lovingly to her temple, by way of encouragement? The mysteries and depths of the soul are unfathomable! Well, they all returned to normality, peach. Human knowledge has an answer to everything. We shall manage it."

She doesn't believe it anymore. She speaks in a voice which is hardly audible, but which is not yet the voice of resignation.

"I thought it was enough just to have a heart."

"Of course, peach. Dr. Klaps mentions the heart very favorably in his preface."

"He speaks about it as if it were the liver or the spleen."

"So you see, he doesn't underestimate it."

"I don't want the heart to be mentioned only in a preface!"

"I assure you that science will sort you out completely, peach. It has made such progress. You'll see, they'll even invent something absolutely new. . . . *They'll invent love.*"

"Do you really think so?"

"Yes, of course, one day they'll invent love. Not just that deplorable phenomenon that makes the earth pullulate with mosquitoes, scorpions, spiders, vipers, hyenas, jackals, and Chinese."

34.

You Can Make Love
All by Yourself

It is exactly as these prophetic words are pronounced that
Johann arrives with a can of gasoline. As soon as he sees
Lily, it is as though the princess of the legends, the madonna
of the frescoes, has stepped down from her illustrious tapestry to draw near to the humble people. It makes him
tremble, our Johann, he takes off his straw hat, he presses it
to his heart, he bows respectfully, a smile of sweet imbecility
spreads over his face, and his eyes are filled with an expression of such hope and tenderness that the little birds start to
sing, flowers to bloom before one's eyes, the streams murmur
something very Virgilian, the entire earth seems touched
by a saintly simplicity.

"Look, the gardener," Florian grumbles.

"Oh, madam!"

For once, Lily doesn't seem well-disposed. "What does he
want from me?"

"What do you mean, what does he want from you? This
is a democracy, he undoubtedly has the right to get it too!"

"Oh, no, not him!"

Florian is shocked. "Lily, that's not nice. If you're going
to start discriminating!"

"I said no!"

"Now, do listen, Lily! That's going too far! It *is* the people! It's good, it's cheap too, it's sacred, it's praiseworthy. One doesn't argue, one accepts it! And nobody will mind. It's well thought of."

"No!"

Johann shrinks all over. His expression is hurt, outraged, his eyelids begin to blink, he's on the verge of tears, dismay, humiliation. He distresses me. I think Lily has no right to spurn the common people. She does wrong to seek the gifted individual. She ought to try the masses.

"Why not me?" asks Johann, despairingly. "Why everybody else, and not me?"

"No."

"Lily, what's all this inhibition about?"

"But what have I done to the good Lord?" Johann wails.

"I don't want to, so there!"

"You must be class-conscious, Lily! It can't be true."

She stamps her foot. "The people, it's always the people, I've had enough of it!"

"But that is where real genius is to be found, peach. That's where all beauty lies. Jesus was a carpenter's son, he started from nothing!"

"No."

"I beg you! I implore you!"

He falls on his knees, our Johann. He clasps his hands. "I want to die happy, like all the others! I'm ready. I'm clean. I've washed my feet!"

"Oh, Lily, do you hear that? He's washed his feet. It's too touching."

"I don't want to, I tell you!"

"But I'll do anything you want me to! Absolutely anything! I'll kill for you, I'll obey orders, I'll march in step! I'll do twenty years' military service if you want. I'll volunteer for everything! I'll go anywhere and get killed, for anything! You can ask me to do whatever you want, you know you can! I'll follow wherever I'm led! I love you!"

"Lily, you must not despise the man in the street."

"I'm a son of the people!"

"Come, Lily, for the sake of the people!"

"I'm a socialist!"

"D'you hear, Lily? He's a socialist. He really has the right to be screwed!"

"Stuff!"

Johann starts to sob. He rubs his eyes with his knuckles. "But why? What's wrong with me? I don't want to feel rejected. It's unfair! I've got a mother too, and she loves her son very much!"

"You hear that, Lily? You can't do that to his mother."

"Fiddlesticks!"

"Have pity, I too have longings!"

"Lily, you can't treat a human being like this."

"But who does he think he is? What does he take me for?"

"But why?" laments Johann. "At least tell me why it's for everybody else and not me. I'll be the laughingstock of the whole village."

"It's really unbelievable, you'd think they take me for a nymphomaniac!"

"No, no, of course not, peach. They all want to make you happy."

"Yes! Oh, yes! I only want to give you happiness! I'll do anything for you!"

This time she looks interested. "Absolutely anything?"

"Yes, anything! I'll flinch from nothing, no matter what it may be! You only have to give the order! I have such a longing . . . such a longing!"

"You hear, luv. This boy wants to make good."

Lily is touched. She smiles kindly. Basically, she hates hurting people. "All right. Go ahead."

Johann gets up. He hesitates a little.

"Well, don't just stand there. Go ahead! Show us. But at least, let it be beautiful."

"All by myself?"

"Yes, all by yourself."

"All right. I'll go. I'll show you how I can love!"

He seizes the can and drenches himself in gasoline. I am rather surprised. So is Lily. Her curiosity is aroused.

"I don't know that trick."

Johann takes a box of matches out of his pocket. He smiles.

"You'll be proud of me!"

"All right, all right," says Florian. "But go a bit further away if you wish to play with yourself!"

Johann dashes into the bushes. Almost at once, I see the blaze. He burns very well. Lily claps her hands, like a child.

"Oh, Florian, look! What a fire! What lovely flames!"

Florian is impressed. "Yes, he knew how to express himself, that fellow. You see, luv, you mut never despise the little people. They sometimes have great inner resources. The true heroic spirit and desire for sacrifice."

The flames dies down rather quickly. Lily watches the black smoke for a moment, and weeps. Florian takes her hand.

"You mustn't cry, luv. Apparently one doesn't suffer, one even feels a kind of ecstasy. . . . Don't cry."

But she is inconsolable. "It's over already! So quickly! Oh, Florian, why does it always last such a little time?"

"Alas, peach. But don't be upset. There will be other heroes to keep the sacred flame burning. Come, luv. We'll go over there and observe a minute's silence. We must encourage the spirit of sacrifice. Come, luv."

He pushes her gently toward this hallowed spot.

I hesitate a little: there is still some gasoline left. But the fire would have no effect on me. I no longer have what it takes. All there remains of me is my old Jewish hope that one day humanity will be created. That she will emerge at last from the old primeval ocean where she is still dreaming her confused dream of a spiritual birth.

One day the world will be created and only then the word *brotherhood* will mean something other than an offer of partnership in guilt and shame.

PART
THREE

THE
TEMPTATION
OF
GENGHIS COHN

35.

The Trap Opens

Something is happening. For the last few minutes, I have been sensing a sinister threat, though its exact nature eludes me. All I know is that I'm beginning to feel at home here, surrounded by friends, and that I see nothing but compassion, tolerance, and good will everywhere. The Forest of Geist is glowing with ecumenical spirit, each branch is an outstretched hand.

This atmosphere of security and acceptance is so strong that my instinct of self-preservation awakes at once. All my fears and suspicions return and, as I look around me with the utmost wariness, the whole illustrious Forest of Geist echoes with the most insidious and treacherous melody of their whole repertoire: *Come along, Cohn, be one of us.*

The danger is terrible. I am the object of a particularly diabolical and deceptive temptation, to which many Jews have fallen prey, with the result that no one has ever heard of them again.

It is no longer a question of suppressing me physically, but morally and spiritually, by "fraternizing" me, and thus forcing me to shoulder the collective responsibility of the species, which would have, among many other grisly consequences, that of making me responsible for our own extermination.

Tfou, tfou, tfou.

I immediately adopt my historical attitude of self-defense: the dark, evil eye, the hooked nose, the hairy, grasping paw, the servile back, the thick, lustful lip. With lightning speed I conform to the caricature of the lowly kike which has always saved me, *Gott sei dank*, from taking part in their holy crusades, from torturing, burning, destroying, oppressing, and murdering. Taking on instantly my protective coloring, I am turning myself from head to foot into the traditional image of Judas—traitor, such as it has been enriching the Christian cultural heritage since the first crucifixion. They're not going to give up centuries of artistic treasures, including all the Renaissance, of which my hateful appearance is such an essential part, just for the sake of having me in Vietnam or elsewhere.

I was not mistaken. For no sooner have I finished disentangling myself from their brotherhood, which had landed on my head with a thousand tons of pity, a hundred grams of pardon, ten cents of forgiveness, a pound of compassion, one love song, a milligram of honor, a bit of napalm, six pairs of French electrodes for Algerian testicles, one Ouradour-sur-Glane, three wise men stealing gifts from a stable in Bethlehem, a Messiah running away as fast as his legs will carry him, a Mona Lisa still soliciting with her dirty smile, one French grandeur and the roundup of Jews in Paris by the French grandeur of 1943, a new German awakening, and a can of gasoline for self-sacrifice but a great deal more than gasoline will be needed to cleanse their brotherhood, when I see Schatz leaping right into the middle of our immortal Forest of Geist dressed in a superb uniform of our ally, the new Wehrmacht, peace be to our ashes. By the way, did you know that right up to the last moment there were some among us who never believed that the Germans would really do *that* to us? We just thought that they were merely anti-Semitic.

As soon as I see Schatzchen all dressed up in German Renaissance, I lie flat on the ground and play dead. A Pavlov reflex.

"Cohn, where are you? Terrific news! You have been accepted. The German people have decided to forget all the harm the Jews and their scurrilous propaganda have done us in the last twenty years. More than that: the Kiesinger Government is about to come out in favor of a mass immigration of Jews into Germany. There are only thirty thousand living Jews left here right now. This is not enough to provide Germany with an ideology, a historical mission. We need at least a million Jews for our national conscience and soul to reawaken. One feels today in Germany an apathy, a lack of ideal, of purpose, which are painful to see: *the Jews have simply got to come back.* If Israel agrees to let them leave, we are ready to exchange ten thousand trucks against them, thus making good the deal Churchill turned down in 1943!"

The saddest part is that the Jews are on my back too, trying as hard as the others to convince me. They are not even pleading: they are furious, indignant, and they try to snatch the yellow star from me, with incredible cheek, a real *Yiddishe hutzpeh.* I've never liked the Jews that much either, let it be said confidentially, there's something human about them, and anyhow, you see, the Jews have given us Jews enough trouble.

"Cohn, are you *mishugeh?* They offer brotherhood, a hundred percent, and you turn it down? Traitor! Judas-shit!"

They are all mad at me, the Jews, they're looking at me with hatred, they want to get rid of me. I wouldn't be surprised if, in the process of becoming human a hundred percent, they had become twenty percent anti-Semitic.

"Cohn, you *ganif,* one has no right to refuse brotherhood and equality! On your knees, accept it, and with tears of gratitude in your eyes. Kiss their hand and say thank you! You'll be able to do everything they do and do it better! You will have your own army, your own *Blitzkriegs*, your own Rommels, and one day, maybe, who knows, your own Napoleons and Hitlers! This is brotherhood, man! Grab it! Haven't you heard the news? They have declared that you are not to be considered guilty of killing Jesus, peace be to His ashes! They are broad-minded."

"But it's worth nothing, their crap!" I yell. "It makes me sick! It's soaked in blood and napalm, it's full of hate, of rotting corpses, burned villages, and murdered kids! Who wants that?"

"Take it, you half-wit! One doesn't argue with brotherhood! One accepts it on one's knees! Grab it! You'll be part of the family! It's the best deal you've ever been offered! Go on, take it! It's pure gold!"

"No-n-no! It isn't worth a cent!"

"That may be, but they're giving it to you for nothing!"

"What d'you mean, for nothing? Blood on my hands, that's the price I'd have to pay!"

"But it won't be Jewish blood, for once! Don't you understand? Your troubles are over! From now on you can even be a Nazi and a gentleman yourself, if you wish! You'll even be able to have your own Gestapo, your own bomb, if you wish! Cohn, from now on you'll be second to none and equal to all!"

I try to summon to my aid the ghost of my much-beloved old master, Rabbi Zur of Bialystok. I've never needed his advice so badly as in this hour of mortal peril. Thereupon I suddenly remember that Israel has concluded a cultural pact with Germany and I almost die of shame at the thought.

I see myself surrounded by Nazis in uniform, flags unfurled, Schatz parades at their head, and suddenly I see a ray of hope. Perhaps this is a flare-up of anti-Semitism? Perhaps they are only going to massacre me?

Not at all. The new Nazis spring to attention and shout triumphantly:

"The-Jews-with-us! The-Jews-with-us!"

"No-o-o!" I yell. "*Gevalt!* Help!"

"*Sieg heil!* The-Jews-with-us!"

They dip their banners at my feet. They try to present me with a swastika.

"The-Jews-with-us!"

Schatz goosesteps toward me, brotherhood on his grinning lips, arm raised in salute.

"Cohn! Great news! *We are all brothers!*"

My hair stands on end.

"*Rakhmones!* Pity! Anything, but not that . . ."

"We are all brothers!"

"*Gevalt!* Enough of your atrocities!"

He opens his arms: "Cohn, come along with us! It won't cost you anything, it's always the others who pay! You'll be doing good business!"

"A business like that, I wouldn't wish it on——"

I haven't even the time to finish my sentence. Brotherhood rises from all sides and the stink is such that I am overcome with longing for the sewers of the Warsaw ghetto. Not one bit of their history is missing from the first crucifixion to the current ones, Stalin rushes and sticks his tongue into my mouth, I invent slavery, crusaders make room for me, St. Louis shows me how to wipe out a population in the name of God, Simon de Montfort teaches me how to take a newborn heretic baby by the heels and smash its head against the walls of Toulouse, I guillotine right and left, and thereupon de Gaulle officially places me next to France on their historical tapestry, among their other golden legends, by proclaiming, on November 17, 1967, that the Jews are "people of the elite, self-assured and domineering." I shout "Vive l'Empereur," I'm made Marshal of France, standing knee-high in corpses.

"No, no!" I yell indignantly. "France for the French! Give it to de Gaulle, he can have it!"

I try to tear myself away, to remain a kike, a stinking billy goat, to save my dignity. But there can be no more doubt, these are my last moments. *I begin to feel I have a historical mission to fulfill*—and the idea is so frightening for a man who has been the target of so many historical missions, that I begin to vomit.

"We are all brothers!"

I cover my ears. I don't want to hear it. Brothers? I'll tell you what it is. It's anti-Semitism, that's what it is.

36.

A MENSH

My indignation is such that all my strength returns to me and I fight my way through the Forest of Geist, hollering, kicking, clawing, falling, dragging myself on all fours, trying to get out of the reach of their brotherhood, till I can no longer hear the recruiting sergeants trying to lure me, Moshele Cohn, of Nalewki Street, the well-known *Yiddishe Khokhem*, onto their bloody historical tapestry, where no Jew has ever been admitted before.

I crawl under some bushes and already begin to feel safe, when all of a sudden I find myself face to face with a man who looks just as scared as I feel. The fellow is almost completely naked and appears to be half-dead. I observe him with a wary eye, but he gives me a surly, nasty look. *Gott sei dank*, this is not a well-wisher. His face is vaguely familiar to me. We stare at each other with intense dislike.

"You wouldn't have some clothes to lend me, would you?" he asks in Hebrew. "One day, I'll repay you a hundredfold."

"Who are you and what are you doing here, stark naked?"

I notice that he is terribly thin and that his whole body is covered with bruises and sores; his forehead is bleeding.

"The bastards!" he growls. "They've been waiting for me for centuries, so they were ready. As soon as they saw me returning at last they organized a reception committee for me. What with my portraits on all those Byzantine icons and reproduced everywhere, the police recognized me at once. As soon as they realized who I was, they got out an enormous cross, even bigger and heavier than the first one, and before I knew, they rammed a crown of thorns on my head."

I go *ts-ts*, shaking my head. I feel moved. I've always had a great respect for Him. He too had dreamed of creating the world. He notices my yellow star.

"You shouldn't wear it like that, openly. Sets you apart. Very unwise."

He knows what He is talking about; He is even more threatened than I am.

"I shouldn't have come back," He mutters, with a heavy sigh. "But I wanted to see how it had turned out. I thought that two thousand years of Christianity would have brought some changes."

I am overcome by pity. "Didn't You know?"

"No, I didn't. If I could have foreseen it, I would have remained a Jew. It was not worth being crucified."

"Now, now," I say soothingly. "Without you, there wouldn't have been the *quattrocento*, the Roman or the Gothic, nothing but barbarism until the impressionists and the cubists. You have played an important part in culture, You see."

He is not listening to me. He seems to be still in a state of shock after all the things He has seen, truly indignant.

"I've been all over the world, since I came back," He says. "I would never have believed that crucifixion would become a habit. Nobody even notices it any longer."

"How is it that this time You were able to slip through their fingers?"

"I still have my ways, as you may imagine. But they almost got me. When they realized that I was not going to let them nail Me to the cross a second time, they started yelling that I was an impostor, but instead of leaving Me in peace, they

wanted to drag Me by force toward the cross, under the pretext that I was a false Messiah. Some logic. You can't win,
with people like that."

"What do You mean to do?"

"I'm going to steal some clothes and I'm going to Hamburg. I shall try and find a boat to Tahiti. I'm told that
Tahiti is the earthly paradise, so of course, it would never
occur to anyone to look for Me there. By the way, to whom
have I the honor?"

"Cohn," say I. "Cohn, Jewish comedian from Nalewki
Street. I was also fairly well known at Auschwitz. I don't
know whether You heard about the place . . ."

His face clouds over. It's rather a hard face, severe, very
beautiful in its primitive ruggedness.

"I know exactly what's been happening," He says. "I've
been reading the papers. That's why I categorically refuse
to try and help them again. Too much is too much. They'll
never change. All it would result in would be a few more
orders for the museums."

He's right, as usual. Hardly has He finished speaking,
when I hear furtive steps in the bushes, and hurried breathing. He has heard it too. It's drawing nearer. I begin to wonder if it isn't the police, when the branches part and I see
the sinister mugs of Michelangelo, Leonardo, Cimabue,
Raphael, and *tutti-frutti,* all of them with paints and brushes
ready and their faces slit from ear to ear with greedy smiles.
The *Mensh* jumps to His feet with a roar, seizes a stone, and
hurls it at Cimabue. Michelangelo and Leonardo break into
a flood of excited Italian, but He picks up more stones, aiming with miraculous precision, and I do my best to help Him.
Leonardo is hit in the eye, screams *Porca Madonna!* and yells
horribly, Michelangelo has dropped his brushes and is hop-
ping up and down holding his foot. We let them have another handful, they hide in the bushes, but go on whining,

all they ask for is one hour of posing, they don't give a damn for the rest, one hour of posing on the cross, for Culture's sake, He has no right to refuse. But they've got hold of the wrong man. They've painted Him so many times as a weakling, docile, sweet, effeminate, full of acceptance, that they've ended by believing Him to have really been like that, as mild as a lamb. They are mistaken. His face is so strong, so severe and virile, and His eyes of such hardness that to see Him is to understand to what degree both Jesus and the Jews have been betrayed and misrepresented, and how deeply centuries of art have sunk into fakery and falsehood. He is a *mensh*, a real one, and there is no trace of acceptance or submissiveness on His angry face. He lets loose a flood of anathema which makes the whole Forest of Geist shake with horror, so unused it has become to archaic forms. Then He flings a few more stones at them, aiming with miraculous skill, and then takes to His heels, while I try in vain to follow Him, with my so much more limited means. I slow down, fall back, paying the price of my exhausting day. He retraces His steps and helps me on. I tell Him, no, please, leave me and run, save Yourself, we mustn't be seen together, if men find out that I have helped Jesus to escape from the cross my name will be Judas to the end of all time.

37.

Colonel Cohn

How long did I lie thus, without thought or feeling, as though they had at last managed to exorcise me, and to free their conscience and memory of my presence? I don't know. However, when I open my eyes, I feel I am a different man. I still remember my past terrors, but now they seem futile to me, as though I had mysteriously changed during my sleep. A strange sensation of having been taken care of, reeducated, morally rearmed and spiritually helped. I feel that I am loved, surrounded by firm friendships, by innumerable intellectual supports. UNESCO, the League of the Rights of Man, the Nobel Prize for two Jewish writers, concerts everywhere, a million visitors a day in our museums, those are the good things I am thinking about, things one *must* think about. What was the matter with me, only a little while ago? A passing weakening of the moral fiber. Let's take a deep breath of Culture and it won't happen again: the air of the Forest of Geist always does one the utmost good, all our invigorating spiritual winds blow there.

I get up and immediately notice something very odd: they've pinched my old Auschwitz clothes. I am now wearing a kind of green uniform with camouflage spots. Hmmm. Strange. How did it happen? What does it mean?

I nervously look for my yellow star: no yellow star. In its place there is a kind of label with something written on it.

It reads: *Colonel* Cohn. I rub my eyes: but here it is, Colonel Cohn, U.S. Army. Strange. Obviously, some mistake. Luckily the yellow star is still here, at my feet. I pick it up and put it back in its place. All is well.

I part the thick bushes and peer cautiously through. I notice immediately that there is something afoot, though I don't quite know what. The Forest of Geist has grown higher, it is bathed in glorious light and glows with noble promises. The flowers smell so good that I can no longer smell anything else. The green grass has grown all over our sores and hides everything one ought not to see, a thousand doves make offerings of peace and love, unicorns and muses gambol everywhere, the historical ruins are displayed with the happiest effect, the sky is of such radiant purity that one gets the impression of an act against nature. There are romantic gazebos everywhere, horns of plenty, lyres in every corner, laurels suspended in the air and ready to fall on your head at the moment of apotheosis. The whole place smacks of their greatest work of art, *Universal Love*. The cultural Renaissance is of such magnitude that there is no place for blemishes, for intrusions: millions of African and South African children could come and die of malnutrition in there without the eye being disturbed. Never have my thoughts been more noble, more high-flown. Where am I? Could I, poor Jewish dybbuk, really have fallen at last into God's subconscious, or perhaps even into that of de Gaulle himself?

I hear the trumpets of glory, I see the plump little angels frolicking all over the tapestry, with nice clean little pink bottoms. Celestial choirs ring high and pure, but it's a real miracle: this time they don't come from heaven, they rise from the earth. The voices are so crystalline, so free from hatred and warlike tones, that the hope dawns on me that half of mankind has been castrated at last and the other half sings its gratitude for this act of mercy.

Or could it be that Lily has been satisfied at last?

I can't see our fairy princess right now. But she is surely here, in the Forest of Geist, so full of spiritual values, aglow with promises, it's always there that she gets laid. Besides, I can see cops crawling all over the tapestry. It's a sure sign of her presence. The guard of honor.

The sky worries me a bit. I have never seen it so radiantly beautiful. One would think that it had not only come closer but that it had reached the earth.

Could it be that the Almighty Himself has come down and satisfied her? It could be. Gerontology is making tremendous strides forward.

Where the devil has she gone and hidden herself? Perhaps to India or to Africa, but what would such a demanding lady want to do in an underdeveloped country?

The air around me is of an intense brightness, white-hot. Suddenly the clouds rise up on all sides and fly away as though affected by some heavenly gallop. Then the sky is clouded by a confused hue, in which the eye guesses rather than sees pulsating shades of pink and copper, as though the heavens were hesitating between dawn and sunset. Nature itself seems to hold its breath.

"Cohn, what's the meaning of that outfit?"

I leap ten feet in the air. It's Schatz. I was so busy scrutinizing the blue yonder—nothing will ever cure me of my old yearning—that I didn't see him coming. He is wearing the same kind of battle fatigues I do, and a helmet with chin strap.

"That's none of your business, I'm American now. I don't have to account to you for anything."

"American? *Mazel tov*. So why are you making that face?"

"We've bombed another South Vietnamese village by mistake. Some dead, some wounded."

"You'll get used to it, that's strictly routine."

"Yes," I grumble. "We can all make mistakes, as the hedgehog said climbing down from the clothes brush."

I stare at my uniform, I touch it, I don't know how it happened, how I got into that.

I hear the most frightful roar above my head, but no, it's not the Almighty coming, it's only some of our jets, all guns blazing.

"Are there any Viets around?" I growl. "What the hell are they doing, those sons of bitches?"

Schatz looks at me with sympathy. "You're making progress, pardner," he says. "You're getting along fine, just fine. You see, once you become one of us, it's not difficult."

There is a little gleam of Nazi irony in the corner of his eye and I don't at all like his patronizing tone. Jews make just as good soldiers as the Germans, and I'm going to prove it to him. They are firing at us from Hill 320, I throw myself flat on my stomach, I crawl along, and what do I see? Four of those red bastards wiping out the boys of the First Company, my best outfit, fuck it!

I grab a grenade, I sling it right in the middle of their yellowness, there's nothing left of them, not one slant eye, nothing but red caviar for red ants! I leap forward, I give orders, I take the initiative, the village is brought to order again, I have a few words of praise for my boys, half of them are Blacks, at first, to be commanded by a Jew made them mad, but I was able to win their respect after three or four villages, and I have even got some Mexicans and Puerto Ricans under me, say what you like, war can be great, it cements brotherhood.

I let out a terrified yell. I wake up covered in cold sweat. I find myself lying with my machine gun among twenty-two Vietnamese corpses, men, women, and children. I must have had a little doze after the fight. There's still a child's foot on my face. I fling it aside, I yawn. I feel dead tired. I notice that I have been made a colonel during my absence and that I'm covered with medals. The billy goat is still there. His tongue is hanging out, and he is soaking wet, Mona Lisa has worked him to death. He is having convulsions, his hindquarters are shaking, he turns toward her, but when he sees that she is still smiling invitingly, he lets out a frightful bleating, tries to drag himself into the bushes, but she has polished him off, he is shaken by one last spasm, he falls over on his back and dies, sprawled out on the ground. The poor beast was no more able to give her satisfaction than all her other lovers, and it would take a damn lot more than Vietnam to make her feel contented at last.

I add up the balance. A dead billy goat, the Mona Lisa's smile, a child's foot: Culture is on my side. My morale is high, everything is ship-shape, except for one thing: what the hell am I doing here in Vietnam, I, Cohn, from Nalewki Street, next to a billy goat killed in action, and one Culture complete with a child's foot and the Mona Lisa's smile? It is the child's foot that worries me particularly. And what if it were a Jewish child's foot? But of course not, it's impossible, still my persecution mania, one can see at once that it's a yellow foot, I don't have to worry.

Anyhow, it's an ideological conflict, so if there are any Jews who have joined the other side they've got what they deserve, those sons of bitches.

I begin to feel lonely here. Where's that swine Schatz? I miss him. I would like to have him beside me. He's a son of a bitch, a former Nazi, but military experience such as his, one's got to respect that, and right now he would be really useful to me. He's a true professional. It would be reassuring to have him with me.

The Mona Lisa continues to look at me with that obscene smile, but no thanks, not after that goat, who does she think I am? She's only got to ask one of them niggers.

But what the hell is Schatz doing? Surely he is not going to let a buddy down? No, it's not possible, it would really be too sickening.

But I have no right to have such doubts about my pal. Say what you like, German soldiers have got fighting in their blood. Schatz has a sense of honor, of comradeship, *Ich hatte einen kameraden.* . . . He'll come and get me out of this.

I am completely exhausted. But I'm not going to let my moral fiber weaken. That's what the Vietcong are trying to do: to weaken my moral fiber.

But what the hell is Schatz doing? It will soon be dark, and the thought of spending the night here all alone doesn't please me a bit.

Perhaps I've not been very fair to Schatz. He had his orders. He's a soldier, he was only doing what he was told.

I would give anything for him to be here.

Something is moving in front of me, in the dark. My heart starts to beat very fast. Schatz? How can I tell? I must whistle a little tune, so that he recognizes me. But what? Something that the Viets don't know, so that he can be sure it's not a trap. I whistle the first bars of the *"Horst Wessel Lied."*

Nothing. It's not him. I begin to feel frightened. Please, God, make Schatz come back! The Viets are surely only waiting for nightfall to pounce on me.

Something is moving again, over there, opposite me, among the ruins. Perhaps a civilian, a wounded man trying to escape? But I can't take chances. I grab a grenade and hurl it, then throw myself to the ground and wait. Nothing. Silence. It stopped moving. I got the bastard.

Schatz has been through the French campaign and the Russian campaign. He's got the Iron Cross. He's a great guy.

I'm sure he isn't going to let me down. Sure, I damn well know I'm a Jew and he's a former Nazi, but that's already ancient history, one must let bygones be bygones. One must be tolerant and learn to forget.

Besides, Schatz is not vindictive. After the war he joined the Foreign Legion, he served the French in Algeria, the French even gave him a medal. I'm sure I can count on him.

Night has fallen now. There is no moon. The goat is beginning to smell.

I'm certain there are Viet patrols around here. If they find me, they'll cut off my testicles and stuff them in my mouth. Schatz told me that's what the *fellaghas* did to the Legionnaires when they caught one of them. I must confess I don't like the Arabs. Schatz killed heaps of them. But where is he? Has he let me down? I can't believe that. I know him. Friendship, to him, is sacred. . . . *Ich hatte einen kameraden.* We're comrades in arms now, he won't let me down. I'm a bit demoralized, that's all.

When the war is over, I shall invite him to the United States. I've got relatives over there. I'll explain to them that he saved my life. They'll give him a good time.

I feel a bit better. I have a terrible craving for a smoke. I shouldn't be using my lighter, but if I hide it under my helmet . . . I had a cigar in my pocket. I look for it, I can't find it. It must have dropped on the ground. I grope around me. . . . Here it is. I stick it in my mouth. . . . God Almighty, it's not a cigar. It's a child's hand.

I let out a howl and wake up, covered with cold sweat.

I look around me with a dazed eye and I am still so frightened that I feel no relief whatever when I realize that Culture is still around and everything is fine, just fine, I have not left the Forest of Geist.

Everything around me is bright and sunny, and I experience such a feeling of belonging, at last, that I try not to look at my hands: there's got to be blood on them. A ghastly vision suddenly throws its shadow over my eyes: Jews parading in Nazi uniforms, shouting *Sieg heil* and saluting a non-anti-Semitic Hitler: humanity transcends the shape of the nose and the color of the skin, each newly accepted brother presses a trigger, throws a grenade, and shouts: Look Ma! I'm human too.

Thank God my yellow star is still there. As long as I hang on to it, there is still a chance. All I need now to feel completely reassured is to see the old sign at the gates to their brotherhood:

JEWS AND DOGS ARE NOT ADMITTED

38.

The Finishing Touch

But what's going on here? I hope this is merely another nightmare, *tfou, tfou, tfou.*

I find myself sitting in the middle of a square. The place is vaguely familiar to me. It is here that the Warsaw ghetto once stood and the Polish kids used to come here to bait me and to make fun of me.

And you know what they're doing now? They're making me pose for the monument of the unknown Jewish hero, the formerly comical, despised *zyd-parch* of six centuries of Polish history.

Now that I am gone forever and the Polish land is free at last of my repulsive presence, they're building a monument to me out of sheer gratitude.

Mitornisht sorgen.

At my feet there's a broken sword and crushed armor: they want me to make a noble sight.

I wouldn't be surprised if there were a few Polish eagles with outspread wings above my head, ready to pounce.

I keep the pose, I don't care any longer. It's all the same to me. They can even put a halo around my head, in the best ecumenical spirit. All right, here's my profile, help yourself. But don't try to straighten my nose. I like it as it is. Chin up? Chin up.

My star, where is my yellow star? Here it is, thank you.

Listen, Mr. Gomulka, I had a friend, could you represent him here, beside me? A black, stinking billy goat. What do you mean, why? A "stinking billy goat," doesn't it remind you of something? That's what they called me, your noble countrymen. Besides, he died trying to make our white Lily happy. Fucked himself dead for our legendary princess. An idealist. All right, all right, forget it.

O.K.? You sure there's nothing missing? What about a pound of culture, a few grams of compassion, one salt shaker, the twisted watering can and six pairs of nice clean socks? Our cultural relics, you know, a few objects of worship left for posterity. They may even be able to start a new civilization with that. *Tfou, tfou, tfou.*

Now, *brothers,* show me where you intend to put me on your historical tapestry. I won't accept just anything, I've had my hour of fame and my minute of silence, even de Gaulle has called me an equal, or, in his own words: "A people of the elite self-assured and domineering."

He seems to have somewhat confused Auschwitz with Austerlitz.

Anyway, I want the best place there is. I'm warning you that if you try to pay me off with the "unknown soldier" *shtik* I'll make trouble for you.

Yes, there, that's not too bad, next to Joseph Bonaparte's light cavalry working for Goya's *Horrors of War* by shooting Spanish civilians. It's a part of the French cultural heritage, you know. Not bad at all.

They're all eager to make room for me, a nice place they're offering, between Charles Martel and Roland de Roncevaux, who fought against the Moors, as they called the Arabs in those days.

However, there's still a gleam of hope, and it comes from France, as usual, when *liberté, égalité, fraternité* show their true faces: one percent of the sons of Joan of Arc, when polled in 1967, approved of the extermination of six million Jews by Hitler, fourteen percent proudly declared themselves anti-Semites, thirty-four percent affirmed that they would never vote for a Jew.

I cling for a second to this faint hope.

Maybe they will let me become a stinking billy goat again, give me back my dignity.

But now the whole historical tapestry is lit by a soft glow. This time, it is not even a glow which comes from the princess of the legends, it is the light of forgiveness and it comes from the madonna of the frescoes.

For, from the highest place of the tapestry and of the whole Forest of Geist, up there, where rises the dome of St. Peter, there comes a voice filled with mercy, and it says: *The Jews are not guilty, they did not kill our Lord and Saviour.*

Mazel tov.

There is no question of hesitating now.

39.

Shwarze Shikse
(concluded)

I find General Schatz at his HQ poring over some maps.
Compass in hand, he is looking for a new angle of attack. He
is right: our legendary princess has been had from all sides,
fucked in every position, one has to find a new way of pleas-
ing her.

"Ah, Colonel Cohn, come in, come in. We can use some
new talent. . . . You're welcome."

I click my heels. "General, sir, just to make sure, is it true
that you have forgiven us all our evil deeds?"

"Positively."

"The revolt of the ghetto?"

"We never think about it, I assure you."

"*The Protocols of the Elders of Zion,* which showed how
we Jews made our *matzo* bread with the blood of Christian
children?"

"Oh, that was merely another golden legend. A creative
work of imagination. A little contribution to our Culture."

"The nose? The ears?"

"With a bit of plastic surgery, it won't show."

"Our Lord and Saviour Jesus, peace be to His ashes?"

"Well, let me put it to you this way: it's not His fault if
He was a Jew. Besides, you did all you could to stop Him."

"Hitler?"

"That was the most wicked thing Jews have done to Germany, we're still suffering from the consequences, but there were so many of you, you couldn't help it."

"We sometimes slept with Aryan women. . . ."

"Whores will always be whores."

"You know that we are merciless, greedy, give us a finger, we take the whole hand?"

"The Germans, too, have been libeled. Look at all the libels people have been speaking about Oradour, about Buchenwald, about Treblinka."

"Marx was a Jew, you know."

"Let bygones be bygones."

"Eichmann?"

"We forgive you Eichmann too. Besides, Germany needs a few martyrs. Who knows, two thousand years from now, Eichmann might look quite different. Colonel Cohn, you see that without reservation we welcome you with open arms."

Just as he utters these words, I see the Baron and the Count pushing their way through the Forest of Geist among the gamboling muses. I must say this for our elite: they know what they're fighting for. The Baron holds on tenderly to his Stradivarius and the Count keeps pointing to the Chagall ceiling for the Paris Opéra, which hovers above his head wherever he goes, a true cultural miracle.

I come suddenly back to my senses once more.

"Gevalt!" I scream. "I don't want any part of it! The ghetto, where is the ghetto?"

No more ghetto, nothing but brotherhood everywhere, dragging me in, deeper and deeper, till I'm covered with blood and shit from head to foot.

"Hitler, where is Hitler? Where are Goebbels, Streicher, Rosenberg? Hey, out there, somebody, make me subhuman again! I don't want to kill no one!"

"Colonel Cohn!" Schatz yells. "You'll be up there with the greatest, with Napoleon, with Louis XIV, with Kaiser Wilhelm, nothing but the best! Take it! It's pure history!"

"Keep your hands off me, you *shmate* peddlers!" I roar. "For Christ's sake, remember we have crucified our Lord Jesus, peace be to His ashes! Please remember that!"

Then, suddenly, I have a bright idea, I see a gleam of hope, which only goes to prove that the skullcap of my well-beloved master, Rabbi Zur of Bialystok, is still watching over me.

"Wait a moment," I say. "This is not the true brotherhood yet. There's still someone missing. Where are the Negroes? I won't take your stuff unless the Negroes are included!"

And I laugh.

But no sooner have I finished speaking when a huge Negro in a GI uniform, chin strap under his chin, his belt bulging with grenades, appears bang in the middle of our historical tapestry, among all our golden legends, his conventional weapon in hand. He is not at all pleased, in fact, he is fighting mad.

"What about me, you bunch of racists? Make room for me, I have the same right to fuck her as everybody else. Kill the bloody bastards!"

They make room for him, delighted to. Schatz shakes his hand, presents him with his own swastika. The Negro is pleased. He knows he can be a Nazi too, now: there is no doubt about it, this is the true, one hundred percent true brotherhood they are offering me.

I take off my pants.

"That's the spirit, Cohn!" Schatz yells triumphantly. "Forward march, into History, with the rest of us! Bang her! Give her a real kick! Kill the bloody bastards!"

I think it over for a moment. "Which ones?" I ask.

40.

Next Please

The light is admirable, the historical tapestry is illuminated with a new splendor: the blood group is irrelevant, it is the color that matters, and here is just the right touch of red for the pure forehead of our princess of the legends, our madonna of the frescoes.

Schatz scans the Forest of Geist through his field glasses.

"Those Chinese mother-lovers are giving it to her now," he mutters. "What if they make her happy before we do?"

I grab the field glasses from him.

"Not with their conventional weapons," I say.

Schatz looks truly awed now. "I didn't know that position," he growls.

"It's Marxist," I say, a bit shattered myself. "Stalin's already tried to make her happy like that, on all fours. He even had a fight with the billy goat over the matter of precedence."

Just as I say these words, an armored column appears bang in the middle of the tapestry, among our golden legends, followed by five hundred bare-assed GI's still wondering what the hell they're doing here.

"The Americans," Schatz shouts, with a gleam of brotherhood in his eyes. "The Yanks are coming!"

"Ha, ha, ha!" I laugh, "you dirty dog, you!"

"The Americans are going to make her happy, sure thing!"

"Happy, shmappy," say I. "It'll be all over before she even knows who's fucking her. They're too quick, too impatient, they're speed maniacs, the Americans are! You've got to give it to her for at least fifteen hundred years before she comes up with so much as the Renaissance!"

I look hopefully toward the sky: nothing, no trace of willingness to come down and give her satisfaction. I'm beginning to think that God should try powdered rhinoceros horn.

I feel a bit sad, for this is the moment of truth, and that is never funny.

"The only way for her to be fulfilled at last," say I, "is to die," and I notice immediately that Schatzchen's face brightens.

"I've always known that Germany still has a historical mission to fulfill," he says.

I hear our trumpets sounding the charge, it's Beethoven, a Vermeer flies forward, leaving a bombed hospital in its track, something hits me in the groin, it's by Michelangelo, the West marches forward bare-assed, and so does the East, each with its system ready, flanked by Freud, Marx, Goethe, the little red book, seventy centuries of the same thing all over again, plus one salt shaker and six pairs of nice clean socks, it's a bargain.

"Grab it, Cohn," everybody screams. *"It's kosher!* It's brotherhood and it's all yours!"

I draw myself up. An immense pride takes hold of me. I raise my head high, I put one foot forward, and to my lips comes spontaneously the great rallying cry of two thousand years of brotherhood:

"Kill the fucking bastards!"

This is a metamorphosis.

My nose straightens up, my ears flatten down, my Judas' face gets nice clean-cut features, I am given an army and strong moral support, a seat at the United Nations and a

Strategic Air Command, a spiritual mission and a historical task, and I quickly recite a *Kaddish* for myself, for the vanishing ghetto Jew who wanted no part of it and who has always been considered as unclean, because he refused to take bloodbaths.

"*Next please.*"

Who said that?

"*Next please!*" the voice repeats, with a nice cultured accent and a trace of impatience.

"What do you mean, next?" I scream.

"Sorry, Cohn," the voice says. "Very sorry, but you are through. You are no longer good material. We writers have to keep up with things, you know. Let's face it: Jewish suffering is rapidly becoming a bit of a bore. Too much is too much. You've been pretty valuable to us writers, but now we have the Blacks and Vietnam . . . so . . . Next, please."

Gevalt! How can he do this to a great entertainer who has been in demand for over twenty-five years? I fight, I holler, I try to hold on to that guy's conscience—it's a smart pro's conscience, it has a nice way with words, plenty of sensitivity and a good following—but what can a Jewish dybbuk do with all these new yellow and black dybbuks queuing up looking for a nice sensitive writer's conscience?

"Listen, now!" I scream. "You don't know what you are throwing away! I'm still best-seller stuff! You know how many copies Steiner's *Treblinka* sold only a year ago? And that other guy's book about Eichmann? You know that one about Eichmann and the little boy? One day, Eichmann——"

"Cohn, who wants to hear another Eichmann yarn? The public is saturated. They had enough of the Jewish *shtik*. Things're happening, you know. They want the Negro *shtik* and the Vietnam *shtik*. You can't keep six million Jews on the best-seller list forever. . . ."

"What kind of talk is this? Anti-Semitism, that's what it is!"

"Cohn, you've got to give up. A writer's got to move on with the times. The anguish and suffering right now are of such variety that even a real pro with a fine, watchful pro's conscience and two secretaries can't deliver quickly enough. The abundance of riches. Even James Baldwin can't keep up with the Negro suffering, though I admit that William Styron's *The Confessions of Nat Turner* has stayed on top of the best-seller list for almost a year. . . ."

"You going to switch to Negro entertainers now, you Judas?" I holler. "Don't you know it's not the color of the skin that matters, it's the talent?"

"Cohn, you're about as much in demand right now as Hiroshima. The public's conscience is busy elsewhere. You've certainly been a godsend to literature and you made people feel good because it is always nice to feel bad about someone, it proves you've got a fine conscience, but you've simply got to come up with something new. Wait till Egypt gets the atom bomb!"

"You can't do that to me, you bastard! I've been the victim of the greatest crime in history. . . ."

"The greatest, the greatest . . . The English say: wait and see."

"Little kids machine-gunned in their mothers' arms . . ."

"Sure, sure, but they're interested in yellow mothers and kids right now. You can't stay on top forever. Look at Charlie Chaplin, Groucho Marx. . . . For twenty-five years you've been getting top billing. I'm telling you, you can be the greatest, they still need fresh talent. That's show business."

"*Mensh,* give me a chance . . . I can still make them laugh."

But I begin to weaken, to fade out, new and eager dybbuks, new blood and fresh talent, are pushing me further and further away. Overexposure. I have been on for too long. *Next please.* I see millions of picturesque dead with colorful exotic backgrounds pouring forward to be turned into bad conscience and good literature. Let's face it: no true pro can afford to lose touch with up-to-date reality and to fall back constantly on the safe blue chips, the Jewish suffering, the Nazi crimes. You've got to keep looking for fresh talent. All the sewers of culture are overflowing with new material and carry me toward oblivion. Talent is queuing up, gathering blood and tears with an expert hand: one must be in time for the Venice *Biennale.* Abstract art triumphs everywhere: napalm does things so well that one can no longer distinguish a nose, a face, a limb; this is surely the end of the figurative period. Chained to his rock, Prometheus laughs hysterically: he didn't know that the sacred fire he had stolen would be used in flamethrowers.

There is one good omen: the dogs remain faithful, look at us lovingly, shake hands. I am moved to tears: a great, unshakable love like that can have incalculable consequences: one day, perhaps, a new civilization will be built on it, indeed, there is a mongrel over there, with soft, gentle eyes: perhaps it will be Him.

I hear a voice very far away and a little laugh, and the voice is so adorable and sweet there is no mistaking it:

"Florian, are they doing all this for me?"

"Naturally, luv. They want nothing more than to make you happy."

"What fire! What eagerness!"

"That's known as virility, peach. Great stuff."

"Florian, who is that gentleman who looks so full of hate?"

"What gentleman? This is not a gentleman. This is a writer, luv. He is trying to get rid of you, luv, of you and all your History. He's trying to get you out of his system, together with your Jews, your Nazis, and all the rest. Passion, see? He loves you, see?"

"Truly?"

"Well, anyway, he loves you as long as he can make literature out of you, peach. He is a pro."

"But then, if he truly loves me, can't he and I . . . ?"

"No, peach. You've had him and he's had you."

"And . . . ?"

"Nothing. Some more literature. A few literary prizes. He can't do a thing for you, peach."

"What's he doing, lying there next to a sewer?"

"He's seeking inspiration, peach."

"What for?"

"He'll probably write another book about you, luv. A book, that's all the satisfaction you can get out of them writers. They're lousy lovers!"

"What's he come to the Warsaw ghetto for?"

"Blood and tears, luv. He's looking for material."

"In such a filthy place?"

"That's nothing compared with his subconscious, peach. A writer's subconscious is one of the filthiest places there are: as a matter of fact, you can find the whole world there."

"Phui!"

"I know. Writers are born shit-eaters, luv, then they use the filth, the horror, and the shame they've eaten to present you with some more literature, peach."

"Florian, isn't there a truly great lover somewhere?"

"Sure thing, peach. I don't want to sound presumptuous, but . . ."

"But you don't want to take me, Florian. You're mean to me."

"I'm not permitted, peach. My employer feels there's still not enough great painting, not enough music, and not enough poetry made out of their suffering, luv. Maybe I shouldn't be telling you this, luv, but you've been created for strictly cultural reasons. As soon as there's enough beauty in their museums, you'll be put to rest. Confidentially, peach, you're the victim of God's strong aesthetic leanings. That is, by the way, the reason for His strong support of the Catholic Church during the last two thousand years. He loves the music, the choirs, the pageantry, and the showmanship. There's no substitute for beauty, in His eyes."

"Who's that angry little man who's trying to swim against the tide?"

"It's only your Jew, luv, always the same one."

"Why's he swimming against the tide?"

"He's that rare kind of Jew who has somehow succeeded in not acquiring the spirit of Christian resignation, luv."

"Why has he painted his face black?"

"He is trying to pass. He thinks that with a black skin he'll be able to keep out of brotherhood, peach. Smart-ass."

"Florian, I am still hopeful. I truly believe that sooner or later they will be able to solve all my problems."

"Sure thing, peach. Remember the charming girl who could only reach orgasm in a fifty-mile-an-hour gale, on the Omaha Beach in Normandy, when the waves were exactly seventy-two feet high and eagles were flying? And the little Frenchwoman from Dijon, who could only make it on the green fields of Waterloo, and the one who could only blossom in the presence of a cop giving her a traffic ticket, and the one who didn't even need a man, as long as she could be left alone on top of the Eiffel Tower? Unfathomable, truly, are the depths and mysteries of the human soul. You're a bit difficult, too, but they'll soon find the right system and you'll reach the most beautiful climax since universal love was invented. Happiness is just around the corner. They're working at it night and day. Be patient. Meanwhile, you'll have to make do with Culture. It suits you very well, it covers you from head to foot, except where you don't want to be bothered."

I can still catch a few glimpses of the vanishing Jew carried away by the irresistible tide of the brotherhood, here is Germany singing to Israel *Bei mir bist du sheyn,* and here floats the 1940 smile of the Hasid Jew whom the grinning German soldiers are dragging along by his beard toward posterity: the smile is immortal and the shame is such that we must be approaching eternity. The essence of our brotherhood flows in huge, white, tempestuous waves, carrying within it a promise of even greater accomplishments. Already the Federal Government of Scientists, established by President Johnson himself, comes up with a bright new ray of hope. The nuclear tests carried out so far, and totaling six hundred megatons, have affected our genes so deeply that at least sixteen million children will be born mentally deficient.

Mazel tov. Sixteen million monsters, that could mean another few geniuses, a few more Stalins, Napoleons, Hitlers, Maos, and, who knows, there may even be a new Messiah among them, a new Messiah, born out of the very depths of the sick, fallout-riddled genes of the species, a near Mongoloid and mentally retarded Jesus, who therefore would not be crucified, but acclaimed as a true spiritual Guide and Father, a four-legged Messiah worthy of leading the race of Cain toward even greater accomplishments.

"Don't try to change the subject, you *ganif,* you!"

"Cohn, I have no more room for you. Can't you see that my writing conscience is full? The Negroes———"

"What about the soap?" he yells triumphantly. "Show me the Negro soap. The Jews are the only ones who have ever been turned into soap, this is History, man! The greatest *shtik* of all our repertoire . . ."

Tfou, tfou, tfou. A *shtik* like that . . .

I hear the distant, capricious voice saying:

"Florian, I do begin to feel moved, I really do. But there is still something missing . . ."

"Really, luv? Now, what can that be? They're fighting and killing for your happiness' sake all over the place, so what can there be missing?"

"A great poet, Florian. I can't, without a great poet, I truly can't. It's not enough to have all this suffering and sacrifice, it still takes a great poet to make something exciting and truly worthwhile out of it!"

"There's bound to be a poet in the heap, luv. There always is. You'll have your aesthetic bliss, luv, take my word for it."

I see Him floating further and further away, out of my literary conscience at last, thus making room for another subject, the South American starving peasants, perhaps, or the vanishing African elephant: as a matter of fact, the South American starving peasants will have to wait, the deadline for my Vietnam piece is drawing near, a writer can't have his conscience overextended, you've got to husband your creative powers and your sensitivity prudently: economy in literature, as elsewhere, is an all-important thing.

"Good-bye, Cohn! If at any time you Jews come up with some new material . . ."

"I'll be back!" he bellows, floating on his back in brotherhood beside the little postman without a message of hope, six pairs of socks with nobody inside them, the salt shaker which has emptied its salt on all the open wounds, a dead billy goat, a broken-down culture, two front teeth, and a Mona Lisa's dirty smile that has swallowed everything.

"I'll be back too!" Schatz yells. He raises his arm, shouts the famous Nazi rallying cry: *Nothing that is human is foreign to me!* and sinks like a stone into the semen of the species, thus going back for good to where he belongs.

"Tell me where you'll turn up next, Cohn," I shout, "just in case I run out of material . . ."

"I'm off to Tahiti, you brute!" he bellows. "I guess I need a fresh audience. They're still innocent out there, I'll make them feel guilty for Auschwitz and everything, the bastards, just you wait! Then, as everybody knows, Tahiti is a paradise, so I've got to help them get out of it, and it would never enter anyone's mind to look for me there. The Garden of Eden, that was before my day!"

"All right, Jew, but this time, no matter what, don't try to save them again! Enough is enough!"

He gets so furious that I can hear His thundering voice quite clearly again, and I see His face almost as plainly as if He were back among us: a strong, virile, savage face, with dark, indignant eyes, a true *mensh*, almost exactly the face He had on the Byzantine archaic icons, before He had fallen into the hands of Italian pederasts.

"Save them?" He roars. "The first guy who talks to me about saving huma——"

I lose sight of Him. I've only got His beloved now and it it is much more difficult to rid your conscience of this mythological beauty than of the murdered Jew. Even here, where once the Warsaw ghetto stood and where I came to look for the true face and nature of our princess of the legends, our madonna of the frescoes, she still manages to rise again, unscathed, from the sewers, like a gracious queen who has merely paid another historical visit to her poor and to her dead, and who is already preparing to climb back into her golden coach and drive quietly home to her fairy kingdom, the never-never land where all beauty dwells. She sweetly nods her head in acknowledgment, answers the cries of hunger and agony with a kindly gesture of her gloved hand, pats the head of the little murdered Jewish page who came out of the sewer to carry her train, help her to cross the ghetto without a blemish, and take her place once more on the golden tapestry woven with such love by her victims' hands.

"Florian, I sometimes begin to lose hope . . ."

"Well, you shouldn't, peach. We haven't yet exhausted all their potentialities. Who knows, peach, they might come up with another Greco, a new Tolstoy. . . . Why do you think I graced Picasso with longevity? Productive little man. He's still capable of giving you a few kicks. Come on, peach, it's getting late. We must get to Basel before they close the museums. They've got some beautiful Klees there. Klee suits you well, peach. So innocent. By the way, did you know that they've just paid more than a million dollars for a Monet, peach? Bang in the middle of the Vietnam war. You just can't give up hope for a species that has such an admirable sense of values. . . ."

Values—shmalues.

"Oh, look, Florian, there's a furious little man following me."

I can see Him too. Incurable! I would like to get up and meet Him, help Him to carry His burden, but my strength still fails me and I am not even sure that there is enough despair in me to make me care again. I don't know how long I have been lying here, unconscious and delirious, at the foot of this monument, in Nalewki Street where the ghetto once stood, where He was born and raised and where I had laughed and cried so often in His company, at the Shwarze Shikse thirty years ago. He is not in very good shape, to say the least, our Cohn, He has obviously had some more *tsuris*. He is terrifyingly thin, half-naked and famished, and they've already had time to proclaim Him, as de Gaulle put it: "People of the elite, self-assured and domineering," King of the Jews, in fact, once more. They've already crowned Him, indeed, and He looks quite dazed under His thorns, but at

243

least He is still there, Cohn the invincible, Cohn the immortal, *mazel tov*. He is bent double under the weight, but He can still perform, as long as there is an audience, and He obstinately follows His beloved, dragging His heavy cross on His back.

"Florian, who is that furious-looking man with burning eyes, who keeps following me?"

"It's only your Jew, peach. Always the same one . . . You've done Him already. They don't seem to be able to do anything about Him . . . Indestructible. Come, peach. Never mind Him—nobody does. He's never been in anyone's way."